FORGEMASTERS OF THE REALM

ARKAAIN SAVIOR

SNÆBJÖRN

Order this book online at www.trafford.com
or email orders@trafford.com

Most Trafford titles are also available at major online book retailers.

Author Credits: The author penned Forgemasters of the Realm,
The Rendering Wars, and Coronation.

Printed in the United States of America.

ISBN: 978-1-4669-9257-3 (sc)
ISBN: 978-1-4669-9256-6 (hc)
ISBN: 978-1-4669-9258-0 (e)

Library of Congress Control Number: 2013909768

Trafford rev. 05/29/2013

 www.trafford.com

North America & international
toll-free: 1 888 232 4444 (USA & Canada)
phone: 250 383 6864 ✦ fax: 812 355 4082

CONTENTS

DEDICATION

To my late father, Robert. I wish he were alive to see
works of my writings.
I also wish to thank the following people:
Loftur Jens Magnusson (died 2013)
Sígny Águsta Gunnarsdóttir
Dora and Gunnar
Björg Sigurlaug Loftsdóttir
Kristan Hall
Reynir Loftsson and family
Magnús Loftsson and family

PRELUDE

It has been over one hundred years since Agnar had passed on. He was instrumental in bringing the Rendering Wars to an end, and as reward, a tract of land called Blesugrof was bequeathed to his heirs. Agnar, a half human and half elf, fought along with gnomes, dwarves, and humans against the hordes from the north to save the continent.

But the world had changed; the age-old malady of greed and thirst for power had caught up with the populaces. Monarchs of the old were slowly eroding with the fall of chivalry and honor. They were replaced by politicians and bureaucrats while those sovereigns that did survive were doing it with less authority. Bickering and lust for power were the new norm and those populaces that weren't participating were left out. As a consequence, the gnomes, the dwarves, and the elven races were subjected to diminished status within the realm of HearthGlen and had less voice over their own destiny. As the years passed, the little people of the realm were subjected to harsh treatment by the human race; unjust imprisonment, stealing of their lands, and even murders were becoming a norm for being one of the "little people."

Agnar's prophecy was being fulfilled: "The elves, dwarves, and gnomes will vanish. This is the way of the world."

(Domain P., Photobucket Elven Warriors, Unknown)

1

Blesugrof Homestead

Rober ran from the bedroom he shared with Stefan and ran upon his mother, whining about his younger brother. "Stefan won't let me play with his friend," tattled Rober to his mother. "He is strange. I'm going outside to play."

His mother went to the bedroom and was going to scold Stefan. As she was nearing the bedroom door, Stefan was inside, laughing and talking in a muffled voice. She opened the door, and sitting on the floor was Stefan and nobody else. "I see you've been up to that again. You need to grow up. You're seven years old now, and there is no fantasy friend. It is high time that you stop this nonsense. Go out and play with your brother."

"But Traikon is real. I swear it. He told me today that I would be famous when I grow up," responded Stefan with a childish voice.

"Get out there and find your brother and help him to feed the chickens. I think your father needs to create more chores for you boys to do, and stop with this nonsense with make-up friends. Scat now. Do something useful," reprimanded his mother.

Stefan leaped to his feet and ran to the door of the cottage, boasting, "I'm gonna be famous, I'm gonna be famous," almost singing as he spoke.

Ten years later . . .

The Farm

Runar was sitting at the table in his abode with his wife, Björglin, reading an astounding letter from the housing authorities from HearthGlen. He was shaking his head in disbelief as the bureaucrat wanted him to report in person with the deed for Blesugrof. Runar knew what the problem was: the housing authorities were trying to take Blesugrof from their family. Runar was looking old, tired, and dejected. He looked toward Stefan, his youngest son, and then back toward Björglin. She was trying hard not to show her discomfort; as a human married to an elf, she didn't want to pick sides. His elven heritage was behind the political squabble, for it was only elves, dwarves, and gnomes who were required to submit deeds to their properties. The race of man wasn't required to submit anything; it was trying to run the other races off their properties so men could use the land for their personal gain. Blesugrof has been in the family ever since the Rendering Wars ended as the land was bequeathed to his great-grandfather, Agnar, for his service during the war. Björglin was quivering as she heard Runar read the letter aloud.

Hear Ye, Hear Ye

Thou art commanded to report to the housing authorities with deeds and other papers to prove ownership of the land called Blesugrof. If ye do not report within the next fortnight, Blesugrof will be sold.

Shamuric, Overlord
Housing Authority of the Realm

Björglin, with tears in her eyes, asked, "What about our sons? What is to happen to our family? We have only known Blesugrof, not a coven within the elven clan in Woodbranch."

Runar shrugged his shoulders in dismay. "One hundred hectares gone. Greedy. All for what? I knew that it would come to this. Look at the numbers of elves, dwarves, and gnomes which have been bought out, burned out, or swindled in this area."[1]

Björglin put an arm over her son Stefan's shoulder and said, "Can't anyone do anything about this? Strompur and his dwarven family returned back to castle Vokva. They gave up, and now humans live there. And what about the gnome family two farms down, the Lofturs? They had a suspicious fire not so long ago, and they gave up. Humans are now living there too."

Stefan interceded and said, "What about my imaginary friend when I was a young boy? You know,

---

[1]   Hectares: land measurement—100 hectares is 284 acres.

the one who drew pictures for me and always said that he would save us when the time comes? I mean, that was about ten years ago, but I still hear from him. I know it sounds crazy, but what if Traikon is real?"

"What we need is a miracle, not fairy tales my lad," Runar scolded Stefan. "Even your brother never has seen your friend, this Drarkon character or whatever his name is. I don't want to hear another word about this."

"Runar, your son is old enough to take part in this. It is his Stefan's life too." intervened Björglin. "Stefan and Rober are your sons. At least let Stefan have his say."

"Mom is right, you know. Take a look at mom. She can go to the village stores because she is human, and you and I and my brother can't go in just because we are elves! Just look at the sneering and bantering and disgusted way the villagers look upon us! How come Rober can join the realm services? I mean, if we are an enemy of the realm, why do they let us join the service? And what if the service decides to attack elves? Would they order Rober to kill them? Nay, I say. I say nay unto thee. Rober should never kill anyone just because of being elven, a dwarf, or a gnome," exclaimed Stefan.

"This is treasonous talk. We have always lived by the law. This is talking about revolution. There must be a way within the law," snapped Runar.

Björlin, with tears in her eyes, choked out, "If Rober is ordered to slay elves, dwarves, or gnomes,

I . . . I will hide him and help in any way I can to assist him to escape the authorities."

Stefan pointed a finger toward Runar and said, "How many more elves have to be thrown into the debtors' prison? How many have to be arrested for walking on the wrong side of the road? How many unjust laws have to be enacted just to appease the Althing bureaucrats just to oppress the elves, dwarves, or gnomes?"[2]

---

[2] Althing: Government by the people that diminishes royal authority. Elected bureaucrats run the government, not fiefdoms.

Helgi the Grey

There was a knock on the door, and everyone was visibly afraid of who was waiting on the other side of the door. Another knock—Runar snapped his fingers and signaled toward Björglin and Stefan to hide in the other room. Runar cracked open the door to see who was there. "Ah, Helgi, my old friend," he exclaimed as he opened the door to let him in. Helgi the Grey was standing outside, an old human with a flowing long white beard, and attired in his wizard's robes. "Come in, come in, you are most welcome at such times of peril." Runar shouted toward the other room and said, "It's only Helgi. Come out and greet our guest."

Helgi hugged Björglin and shook the hand of Stefan, which was extended outward to him. Helgi, with his staff resting against the table, said, "Björglin, I haven't seen you since what, Þorrablot?" with a twinkle his blue eyes.[3]

"I wish these were happier times for visitors. I'm afraid that Blesugrof is under peril as we speak," said Björglin. She pointed to the letter lying on the table

---

[3] Þorrablot: An annual festival where free-roaming sheep are herded up and shorn for their wool. It is also the time for slaughtering them for their meat. Usually, all the neighboring farms take place in the event.

and added, "We don't know what to do. The world as we know of is going mad."

Helgi was perusing the letter, and after he finished it, he said, "This is sad news. I remember when Agnar was given Blesugrof by King Biggy of the gnomes. It was promised to never leave the family, the rightful heirs of Agnar."

Turning toward Stefan, Helgi asked, "And as for you, young Stefan, where is your brother? I haven't seen you for four years now."

"Oh, Rober—he is getting ready to graduate from the rogue guild in HearthGlen. He is really upset about the restlessness in the elven community, and I hope he deserts the service if he is ordered to kill our own kind," said Stefan. He thought for a moment and added, "Say, how *old* you are anyway?"

Helgi chuckled and winked an eye. "I'm older than the hills, my child. Yes, yes, I knew your great-grandfather as a mere young lad. Tut now we need not talk about me." He bent toward Runar and Björglin and asked, "What do you want me to do? I'll help in any way I can to save Blesugrof. But I must warn you, I have been following closely the troubles in the realm about the dwarves and gnomes. There are powerful forces within the realm which have been working under the darkness for many years. I suspect Svaramin and Mortikon are behind a lot of it. Mortikon so dislikes the dwarves and elves for the alliance during the Rendering Wars. It is easier to fight politically these days without shedding a drop of blood."

Runar was visibly relieved that Helgi was offering his help. "Aye, I thank ye so very much. I have no knowledge of the laws which have been passed, and I *know* they will cheat me. Men have been trespassing of late, and now some of my sheep are missing. I think they intend to scare us out," offered Runar.

Björglin piped in and said to Stefan, "Tell us about this Traikon person. See Helgi if he knows anyone of the name."

Helgi immediately snapped up and shouted, "Traikon—where have you met him? Speak up. If this is the same Traikon that I knew, you will have a great ally. Speak up now."

Runar interceded with "*Björglin*, don't give anyone false hope. He was an imaginary childhood memory—"

Helgi held his hand up to silence Runar. "There are forces within this world that you know nothing of. Anything that is of help will be greatly appreciated." Turning to Stefan, he commanded the story be heard. Then Stefan recounted of how his friend, Traikon, was going to save the elves. Traikon never told Stefan exactly *how* he was going to save the elves, but he did say when the time was right, he would be there. Stefan had never met or seen Traikon, but for years, he had been in contact with him, and Traikon used to spend hours alone with Stefan as a playmate. Traikon always came when Stefan was alone, mostly at night. Stefan then produced a drawing that Traikon insisted is made:

"By the gods, this is an amulet. Powerfully inscribed—it is an Arkaain amulet! I haven't seen one for several hundred years now. And as for Traikon, Runar, he is as real as I am. He has been trying to contact you for years now. The Arkaain is the amulet which contains knowledge of the cosmos. He senses turmoil in the future. Perhaps he wants to save the elves from the encroachment of men. But *why does he not appear himself?*" exclaimed Helgi the Grey.

Runar was dejected and offered an apology to his son Stefan. "I . . . I . . . I am so sorry that I had doubted you. Perhaps . . . perhaps if I had listened to you . . ."

Helgi consoled Runar and said, "What is done is done and not to be undone. Stefan was right to bring his tale out in the open. Don't let this interfere with what is ahead of us. I will meet you in HearthGlen in three days. Do *not* discuss with anyone unless I am in your presence. I still have powerful allies in HearthGlen. Perhaps we can postpone the inevitable." Turning to Stefan, he instructed, "We must go to Woodbranch posthaste and talk to the Gjaldakona, try to find out where Traikon is."[4] He added, "Do not speak of this with anyone. We may still have time for a plan. Remember, Runar—HearthGlen in three days."

---

[4]   Gjaldakona: a witch or sorceress.

Woodbranch Gjaldakona

Helgi and Stefan were mounted on their horses—Helgi on his white stallion and Stefan on his palomino mare—and they were getting ready for the trek to Woodbranch. It was now late, almost sunset. It had been a beautiful day, but it took a gloomy turn for the worse, turning into a dreary day. Stefan was looking about the farm—mostly dirt and stone-constructed abodes with thatched roofs. He was wondering if he will ever see Blesugrof again. He obviously had a pained look on his face, and he was filled with fear. Runar was standing in the doorway and shouted, "May the gods be upon you! Take care of yourself, Stefan! And, Helgi, I'll be in HearthGlen in three days!"

Stefan and Helgi were traveling at night—a cloudless, starlit night—and they had been riding for over an hour. Stefan asked Helgi, "So you knew my great-grandfather? Was he real war hero, or were those stories just fables?"

Helgi didn't respond immediately as if to ponder the question. "Some of the stories I have heard are partly fable, partly true. I know that he had re-united the dark elves and wood elves after the great sword Mjolnir was re-forged. And yes, your great-grandfather did strike the mortal blow that slew Kaldhjarta—Mortikon—that's his name now. Like me, Svaramin and Mortikon have assumed numerous names at different times in their lives. Mortikon is a leiche now after having been a victim of Mjolnir."

"Are you immortal or a god?" asked Stefan in amazement.

"Nay, Stefan, my lad, I am as mortal as you are." Helgi chuckled. "You asked me how old I am. Let me just say that I have a different station in life from other people. I have been called Snjofell, Merlin, and Helgi the Grey, among other names."

Stefan stopped his horse to don his cloak as it was starting to get cold at night. Then he asked Helgi if he had ever met Traikon. "Sire, what do you know of Traikon? Have you ever met him? How can he help us?"

"Nay, Stefan, I have never met Traikon. I only know of him, but I do know that the Gjaldakona knows of him intimately as I have heard. He has some magical powers that are beyond your imagination. I am riding at your side because of the distrust between your elven and human side. The elves and I go back for centuries, and they totally trust me. Let me do the talking. Some of the elves don't want to speak your great-grandfather's name, Agnar. After you have introduced yourself and explained about Traikon, I will excuse myself as I need to go to your father in HearthGlen," said Helgi.

"What about Mortikon and Svaramin? Have you met in battle as foes?" asked Stefan.

"Ah, the question of the ages—yes, I have tested my steel against them many times in the past. But they are not an enemy as you know the term. They are acquaintances, if I may use it loosely. We are combatants but not enemies. Believe it or not, they are men of honor and chivalry," replied Helgi.

Stefan had a confused look on his face and said, "I suppose I will never understand that. I mean, being combatant but not enemies."

Soon the duo was nearing Ft. Hermana and the village. It must have been near dawn as the horizon was brightening. They could hear the town crier going down the street and heard dogs barking. The famous Boars Inn was just waking up from its sleep, and Helgi pointed toward the field off to the right, where Agnar and Helgi drew swords with Orcs. "Gagns—I remember as if it was yesterday. Ah, he was the gnome which was the original owner of Boars Inn," Helgi said. "Mighty fine gnome chap, I must say. We shared many meals in there."

As they got closer, Stefan could read the sign on the front door, "*No Dwarves, Elves, Gnomes, or Dogs Allowed*." "What has this world come to?" asked Helgi. "If it weren't for the little people, the realm would not have survived. Greed and lust for power created this atmosphere, always looking for more power, but they haven't learned how to control it." Helgi spurred his stallion on and said, "Come, my lad. We have about three more hours of riding until we reach Sko Forest."

Soon Helgi and Stefan were entering the Sko Forest. Stefan told Helgi that they were being watched, that his elven senses have alerted him. The elves were being extremely elusive and dared not to contact the intruders in their forest. They rode some distance more, and at midday, Helgi announced that they had arrived at their destination. There were not any homes or campsites as the elves lived in the trees. There was nothing but trees around them. It seemed like an empty forest, and soon Helgi hailed, "I wish an audience with the Gjaldakona." He received no response, so Helgi shouted, "I know that you are here, and you know who I am. I need to speak with the Gjaldakona!" They were met with silence. Again, Helgi addressed the invisible inhabitants, "It is imperative that Gjaldakona show herself. It is about Traikon."

Suddenly, a group of male elves appeared from behind the trees and addressed Helgi. "Why are you here, especially with a half human as company? What do you need with Gjaldakona?" The leader of the group had obvious elven traits with his long pointed ears and eyes slanted upward toward his temple, and he sported silver-colored hair. He spoke with a tone of whispery distrust and disrespect.

Helgi dismounted his stallion and hailed the leader, "Hallo, Laugalfur. We have not met for many years. You know of me, know that I would never bring harm to the elven clans. Was it not me who stood beside your father and his father's father against the horde forces outside Fort Herman? I tell you that your clans are under dire peril, and I *will* have an audience with Gjaldakona! My companion and I are on a quest to save the elves from encroachment by the humans, and we will not be denied."

Laugalfur scoffed. "And what if it is true, this quest of yours? Yes, we were once allied with the humans, but what have they done for us? They lie, cheat, and steal from us. They only bring destruction wherever they tread."

"You are a fool, Laugalfur! You and your people hide in the trees while your own people languish in prisons. Their homes are burned down, they are assaulted, and all you can do is cower in your trees. I and my companion, Stefan, are at least doing *something* for the elven people, not hiding away and hoping that the humans leave," retorted Helgi.

"And you, Helgi, are—" Laugalfur was interrupted by a shout from behind a tree.

"Laugalfur, calm down. I will speak with Helgi and his companion. I already know of what your quest is, and you are right. Traikon senses that if you and your companion do not accomplish the deed, then it will be the end of all elves," espoused the wrinkled old woman known as Gjaldakona.

She is a real hag, thought Stefan. She was a hunchbacked old woman, was squinty eyed, had gray-silver hair, and was leaning on her staff. She cackled, as she snorted through her nose and said, "Laugalfur, just calm down."

Traikon's Request

Gjaldakona escorted Helgi and Stefan into her home—a huge tree in the middle of the coven. There, she introduced herself to Stefan and asked him if knows of the dangers in attempting to contact Traikon. "First, I am elfin like you, and I have not allegiances with the race of men. My mother is human, but we have been raised up as elves. I am Stefan Runarsson of the estate called Blesugrof. My great-grandfather was Agnar from this coven." She grinned slyly and grunted an approval. "I only know of Traikon from my daydreams. I have never seen nor met him. I was told that I should contact him because he claims to be the savior of the elven clans. The time has come to reach out to Traikon. Other than that, I know very little about the ordeal."

Gjaldakona then turned to Helgi and said, "And, Helgi, my old friend"—cackle, cackle—"why have you come to me? What interest do you have in this matter?"

"When Stefan showed me the drawing of the amulet Arkaain, I knew immediately that we needed to seek your counsel. But no one knows where it is, so I beseech you for guidance," answered Helgi.

Gjaldakona cackled and snorted through her warty nostrils. "Yes, yes, come closer, and I will tell what you need to know." Stefan scooted his stool closer to the old hag and waited to hear what she had to tell. Cackle—cackle. "First, I want to ask you some personal questions. Have you ever killed a being—not an animal or a pest—but a living being?" Cackle, cackle. Her right eye opened widely while her left eye stayed squinted. "Have you ever stolen anything of value? Have you ever intentionally lied—not childish pranks—but intentionally lied for personal gain? Do you consider yourself an honorable lad? These things I need to know because you are about to delve into exactly things as such."

Stefan felt as though he were being violated, as if she was trying to look deep into his soul. He looked to the floor and then around the room. It was dark, save for the fire under the pot in the room. The flames from the fireplace danced around the room, giving it an eerie atmosphere. He then replied, "Madam, I am an honorable person, and I was raised up to respect the laws. I am being honest, so no; I have not done these kinds of deeds. But . . . but what does anything of these scoundrel-ish deeds have to do with this?"

Gjaldakona squinted an eye toward Stefan and said, "Because, my lad, if you wish to see

Traikon"—snort, cackle—"these will be required to do: brazenly lie, steal, and yes, even to do murder. Where you will be going, you will only have your wits to save your miserable life, for everything and everyone about you will be trying to shorten your own. Are you up to the task?" Cackle, cackle.

Helgi gasped, *"Northern Realm!"* He had an expression on his face as if he were being asked to confront the demons of the underworld. "He is going to be thrown to the wolves. He cannot be asked to go there alone! He has no soldierly skills. He is just a young lad. At least Agnar had some hunter skills when he was up there. He has nothing of the kind."

Stefan interrupted Helgi with a raised hand and responded with "I . . . I . . . *yes*, I may be young, and maybe I am not a soldiering type, but I will do what must be done. If I have to lie, cheat, and steal, then I will learn, and even murder if the occasion calls for it. I will sell my—" Suddenly, Stefan threw his hands over his head and turned toward the fire in the house.

Stefan asked with a contorted face, "Aye, I hear you. What? Say it again." Stefan was waving his hand in the air as if he were demanding silence. A small pause ensued, and suddenly he stated, "I understand you. You can lead us to where?" A moment of hesitation gripped the room. "Another land—far, far away from here. Aye, I will tell them."

Helgi and Gjaldakona were waiting with baited breath as they knew that Traikon had been in contact with Stefan. "Well, out with it," demanded Helgi.

Stefan then explained, "He said that his children were in peril and that we must leave here soon, or it will be too late. He said that he will lead the elves to a promised land with lavish forests and where there are no humans, a land far across the oceans to unchartered lands where we can flourish as a people. I never heard of any children before."

Gjaldakona sneered and said, "You know not about things of nature in the world. Wise people such as Helgi and I know much, but we know nothing compared with the knowledge of the cosmos as Traikon knows."

Helgi agreed and added, "We must take action soon then. But I will not allow this innocent child to confront the evils of the North Land alone. I insist that you have a party of four—maybe five—before I let you be thrown to the demons of the north."

Gjaldakona smirked and agreed with Helgi. "I suggest a paladin for healing, maybe a priest, and someone with sword skills, such as a healer." Snort. "He can use a rogue too, perfect for stealing and lock picking and skills in stealth mode. It will help if he has someone with skills for negotiating with the dark elves, for his first target is near Outpost Bleakniss just north of the dark elves' covens. I know of such people except for the rogue, but they must be sworn to secrecy, and they must be volunteers. There is a good chance that they may never return." Cackle, cackle.

"S-sorry if I lack any skills such as those, and I surely wouldn't want anyone to volunteer to face death itself," interrupted Stefan. "But what about Rober? Surely he would join. He is finishing rogue guild training now. Can he take a leave of absence to come with us?"

Helgi approved the idea of getting Rober to help. "I must leave within the hour to HearthGlen. I will speak with the headmaster of the guild about getting a deferment on realm services. In the meantime, Gjaldakona, can you help Stefan with some training until Rober comes?"

"Of course, my dear," said Gjaldakona, smiling and with a cackle. "You need to steal the amulet from an old man—a blind man—from his cave in the outskirts of Bleakniss. But he is no ordinary person, so take good care that your thievery goes undetected." Cackle. "The second destination will be the hard part. You are to enter the portal atop Vulkanfjall, but you will need to use the amulet to gain entrance. The areas around the portal are guarded by towers—scrying towers." Cackle, cackle. "One slipup and this task will be for naught, for the minions of the north will surely slay you and your party. And you, Stefan, under no circumstances are you to divulge your task to *anyone*, not even to your own party members. If a single word is leaked out, Mortikon and Svaramin will send their minions down upon you."

"N-n-not even Rober? He is my brother, you know," asked Stefan.

"Especially not Rober! *Nary a word!* And never talk about Agnar, particularly around the elfish clans. They consider him taboo," cried Gjaldakona.

Helgi bid farewell toward Gjaldakona and advised Stefan that he should trust the old woman. "Take good care that you heed everything Gjaldakona tells you. I will have Rober to meet you here. In the meantime, practice your swordsmanship. You will need it."

Gjaldakona turned toward Stefan, squinted an eye, and said, "You will reside with me, my dear, until your departure on your adventure. I will muster your volunteers. One is a dwarf living in hiding here. The other is an elf. He has cousins amongst the dark elves. I think I can find a gnome too—a mage, I believe. Stay here."

HearthGlen Revisited

It was sunrise on the third day. Helgi entered the city; HearthGlen was a city now, not just a capital castle. The town criers were everywhere, jostling the inhabitants awake. Riding his white stallion through the old castle gates, he needed to go off to the left was where he needed to go. The guild sector was where the guilds were located just on the outskirts of the industrial section. The rogue guild was run by a human named Able Shortpils, a noble gentleman whom Helgi had met several years back. Helgi meandered with his steed through the back alleyways and noticed that almost the entire gnome sector was boarded up. There were never many elves in HearthGlen as the elven clans kept to themselves. There was still a large dwarven population in the city as they were always industrious and gregarious by nature. *I hope that Runar is here. Maybe I'll have to look for him, perhaps ask around in the guild,* Helgi thought to himself.

Helgi found himself knocking on the guild entrance and was admitted by a lad of maybe seventeen years of age. Inside, there were several rooms for training. One was for drills in dagger instruction, and the other room was used for teaching lock picking and theft. At the end of the hallway was a door for the students' quarters and another doorway for the office used as the headmaster's lodging. On the right wall of the hallway were display counters that contained the various knives and daggers used as rogue weapons. Able was just coming toward Helgi with arms extended. "Helgi, my friend, I haven't seen you for two years or more. You are always welcome in my place." Able was an unusually tall man, had short brown hair, and was well dressed in his rogue tabard. Helgi sensed that Able was an odd rogue, not sneaky or typically roguish in appearance.

Helgi smiled broadly toward his friend and said, "Able, my friend, I should have been by here to visit much more often, but life takes me to too many places in my chores." Helgi embraced Able and added, "We have much to catch up between friends. And I wish a boon, if I am not too rude to ask. I ask for a terribly important favor."

Able escorted Helgi into his headmaster's den and asked, "And what can I do for you? I am sorely indebted to you for your help in the past. Ask and you shall receive."

"My purpose here is twofold: to help an elf named Runar, the father of Rober, who is a student here, and to ask that Rober get a deferment from service as he is graduating this week. I need Rober to assist with a band of adventurers who are going on a dangerous task. Of the task, I am not in liberty to say," pronounced Helgi.

"Ah, I see. I have already met Runar. He is quartered here since no one will rent to an elf—sad, really—and the gnomes that used to live here are all gone. I have heard all of the hawkers in the streets and the politicians, and I don't like it a single bit! Have you seen the fliers around the city? Our best students were gnomes, dwarves, and elves, but they have fled because of the turmoil caused by the politicians and bureaucrats. Of course, I will grant your wish, no questions asked," Able responded firmly.

Helgi beamed warmly with a twinkle in his eyes. "I will forever be indebted to you for your assistance. Yes, the countryside has been poisoned by the politicians towards the small people. I am certain that Mortikon and Svaramin are behind this. How much do you know about this *Shamuric* character?"

"Shamuric is nothing but a mouthpiece of Sibbi Ljotmann. He does what Sibbi tells him to do. On the other hand, Sibbi is a spiteful, glib politician who will stop at nothing to get his way," responded Able.

"Runar and I have an appointment this afternoon with Shamuric. But first, I need to visit our king, Reynir. Can you tell Rober that we will drop by this evening? Oh, and can you ask Runar to come into the office?"

"Your wish is my command." Able bowed toward Helgi.

Helgi was admiring the bust of Dabbilus in Able's office and recollected his deeds within the Jarnsmiða

Forge. *Life is strange sometimes. Dabbilus was a fine paladin by trade but wound up creating the rogue guild,* thought Helgi nostalgically. On the wall behind the porcelain bust was the shield that Dabbilus carried and his broadsword. He recalled when Helgi first met Dabbilus, introduced by King Magnus in the castle Vokva. *Yes, he was a fine paladin,* contemplated Helgi. He recalled about the good times they spent together, had a pipe and mugs of ale together, talking about life in general. *That was a time when honor, chivalry, and a decent code of conduct were held in high esteem.*

"Ahem, you seem lost in your thoughts," said Able. "Sorry if I disturbed you."

Helgi was shaken from his daydream and turned toward Able, accompanied by Runar and Rober. "Greetings, my friend," said Helgi as he shook the hand of Runar. "And as for you, Rober, look at you. I haven't seen you for a few years now, and you are a fine-looking lad, not a child as I remembered of you."

Rober shook Helgi's hand and bowed out of courtesy. "Sire, it is good that you have agreed to aid us in our times of trouble. From what I have seen and heard here in HearthGlen, I'm afraid for my family. I rarely travel the streets now as the inhabitants have turned against the elven clans. I doubt that you can offer anything more than hope for us."

"Tsk, tsk, now cheer up, my young lad," said Helgi with warm facial features. "Aye, Rober, but I *do* have a plan, one that requires your skills and training. Headmaster Able has agreed to let you defer your service from the guild, but secrecy is of the utmost importance. I may not be able to save Blesugrof, but I am thinking of a plan that can save the elven peoples. I cannot speak of this plan—not even to you, Rober—but Stefan is waiting to meet you in Sko Forest, where he is formulating the plan now as I speak. But you must be a volunteer as it is a dangerous mission, and your tasks ahead will be formidable," explained Helgi.

Rober's pointy ears twitched in excitement, and a smile crept upon his face. "I look forward to the testing of my skills which I have learned here. Aye, I will join you. I will struggle for the elven peoples," exclaimed Rober.

Grinning widely, Helgi acknowled Rober's enthuisasm and stated, "This is settled then! Your father and I have some business in the city, and we shall return shortly. In the meantime, pack up some of your things which you might need on your journey. Sharpen your daggers, arm yourself with poisons, and use your best leather armors. Remember—utmost secrecy. You're not to speak of this with anyone."

Runar and Helgi were destined to the castle to visit the king Aegir and enlist his help. Runar had put his cloak up to conceal his elvish features. Walking through the cobblestone streets, they couldn't help but hear from a street hawker. The pudgy, ugly midaged man with a distorted face full of hate was standing on a crate with his arms flailing about and was lecturing the crowd around him.

Never forget Fort Windswept and the valiant knight Stephan. He died for me and you! The disgusting gnomes betrayed us after everything we humans had done for them. The elves are the worst! Down with the elven clans! They cursed us and turned their backs to us. How much treasures and blood were lost because of them? How much longer do we need to have them around? They are nothing but tree huggers, swinging from the branches.

"Misguided fools," spat out from Helgi's mouth. He guided Runar around the street hawker and the crowd of two dozen but spoke no more about it. Helgi knew about the fall of the fort. He personally knew Stephan, and his audience knew nothing of the Rendering Wars. It goaded him terribly to listen such rubbish. Changing the subject, Helgi remarked, "Looks like snow pretty soon." He received no response from Runar. He knew that he was trying to console Runar. He glanced back toward Runar and could see the cringe that emitted from his face. Runar was quickly getting despondent, so Helgi stopped walking, turned, and put both hands upon Runar's shoulder. "Runar, I am so sorry about Blesugrof, unhappy that you have been adorned with the problems in society. But I tell you now, feeling dejected and sorry for yourself is not the answer. There are plenty of humans here, right here and now, that do not agree with the direction society has taken. This is the way of the world, and nothing neither you nor I can provide easy answers. I will not abandon you, your family, or the elven clans."

Runar looked into Helgi's eyes, and he could see the caring and truthfulness emitting from Helgi. With a remorseful voice, Runar said, "Aye, Helgi, my eternal friend, what you say is true. But what if your plan goes afoul? I stand to lose not only Bleusugrof but my two sons as well. Aye, I have been laden with not just my problem but the problems of society as well. How do you not see that I only wish my situation would just go away?"

"Aye, I do indeed see your situation. But what about Björglin? Does she not lose anything? Do you think she has the same problems weighing upon her shoulders? She is an outcast, both from within the elven clans and the human race. And what about the elven clans? If they do not face up to the real problem, they will be hunted down for their lands. Nay, my friend, even if we save Blesugrof, do you think it would be over? Do you not think that they would drive you away so they can steal your lands? Is it not better to die in combat or as a cur scurrying about as a thief in the night? This plan of ours *must* work. This is combat, as real as meeting swords on the battlefield. Only this time, Svaramin and Mortikon have changed the game rules. They are dividing the races so they can conquer them all, one bit by one."

Runar gulped a breath of fresh air. "I will do what I can to bring the plan to fruition. I now have thought that my problem—nay—*our* problem is seen in a different light. Aye, Helgi, my old friend, of course you are always right. Thank you for being honest and forthright with me. I was thinking 'Woe is me' without thinking of others in the predicament. And aye, I do think that the weather is changing."

Helgi and Runar stood inside the magnificent greeting room of the castle HearthGlen. It was a monument of the heroes that served the realm over the ages. There were superb marble statues of the kings and the knights who fell in combat for the realm, honoring those that tried to defend the way of the kingdom. They could see that there were castle guards in the room, dressed regally, bearing staffs and donning sheathed swords. Their helmets were resplendent with the flumes from various birds in the kingdom. At the end of the hallway sat King Aegir with his counsel, Jon Eskew. The king was a strikingly handsome man, about thirty years of age, with lucid blue eyes and short blond hair.

As Runar and Helgi walked and reached the red carpet's edge, they took a knee and bowed toward the king. "I am at your service, Your Majesty," announced Helgi.

"Helgi of my old companion, stand up. Come and greet me as a true friend," responded the king. "And who is this with you? I haven't seen you for almost a year, my friend Helgi. You are most welcome in my house."

Helgi introduced Runar to the king, announcing that Runar was the great-grandchild of Agnar from Blesugrof. "Do the exploits of Agnar not evoke tales from your great-grandfather, the king Baldur? Surely Agnar was oft mentioned in these halls from the past."

"Aye, I have heard many stories from Baldur and my father. I know of this farm of yours, Blesugrof," said the king to Runar. "And what brings you here? How can I be of assistance to you, honorable Runar?"

Before Runar could respond, Helgi raised a hand and asked the king if he could speak forthrightly. "I'm sure that the events of late have not eluded you within the kingdom. I wish to address the grievances of the populace. I am asking for a godsend from you, Your Highness. I do not want you to be offended, and thusly I ask you with humbleness that you grant this boon."

"Aye, Helgi, I have noticed the happenings within the kingdom. Please, disregard your manner of speaking with me. Speak to me as a friend. Let us take a walk in the castle gardens. I too wish to speak with you freely. Runar, please, I ask you too to be straightforward. A friend of Helgi's is a friend of mine."

The king removed his crown and gave it to Jon and then donned a cloak as the weather was cooling rapidly. The king escorted Helgi and Runar out into the castle gardens, a magnificent structure to behold. There were fountains spewing streams from marble statues, peacocks strutting their tails, apple trees, and a myriad of flowers galore. "My friend, I must confess that I am no king," the king said toward Helgi. "Baldur—now he was a real king. My father, to a lesser degree, but I have failed miserably as a king."

Helgi was shocked to hear the king confess his honesty with them. "I don't consider you a failure. The world about us is changing. It is as the way of the cosmos. We have different stations in this world, and we are victims of circumstance of change."

"Nay, Helgi and Runar, hear me out. I have little authority or power now. I suppose that I failed to recognize events as they unfolded, but before I knew what was happening, my world as a monarch was being chipped away until I was powerless. I supported the people of the kingdom, the creation of the Althing, supported giving power to the masses. Little did I know that I lost my authority, that I was losing my ability to influence the peoples of this kingdom. Without authority, leadership is impossible. Great leaders *earn* their respect. Authority is not given. I am nothing but a pawn in the kingdom now, just a figurehead living a lavish life but powerless to do anything of consequence. I suppose that I am more a prisoner of my own making. I can't take a walk in HearthGlen. I cannot visit friends lest they come to the castle. Everything in my life is regulated. I'm suffocating now with no freedoms of my own," sorrowfully admitted Aegir. The king seemed to age visibly as he confided his thoughts to them.

Runar said, "You sound like you are lonely, with a few friends, surrounded by spies and enemies."

Aegir placed a hand upon Runar's shoulder and added, "Aye, my friend, a lonely man, older than a man of my age. And spies—I can only count on one hand the people I can trust. All of them are spies or cutthroats."

Helgi then interceded and said, "This is the work of Mortikon. He placed the poisoned dagger in the hands of the Althing, slowly working the dagger into the heart of the kingdom. He is dividing the kingdom, using racial difficulties. I observed on my way here to HearthGlen that almost all the gnomes have fled or been incarcerated. The elves are next, then the dwarves. I do not wish you to usurp your judgement, but can you not regain some of your allegiances with the subjects?"

"Nay, Helgi, I no longer have authoritiy to make peace treaties, make war, dispatch soldiers anyplace. So as you can see, I am in a dungeon of my own making," responded Aegir.

"Sire, I do not wish to be rash, but I was hoping that you could intercede with the closing of Blesugrof. I am currently working on a plan to save the little peoples before they lose their lands. I am not of liberty anymore for the moment, but if you could delay the loss of Blesugrof for a few months, it would help with our plans," asked Helgi.

"Of course, I will help in any way that I can. And I will keep it to myself—about the plans you are making—as there are few in the city I trust," responded Aegir.

"Can you not address your subjects?" asked Runar. "I mean, might you not speak directly to the populace, work around the Althing?"

"Nay—alas, it might make the situation worse," answered Aegir. "If I had some type of proof that Mortikon were involved—but if any bureaucrats are in league with him, then I can move against them. Otherwise, I'm afraid it would be a useless attempt."

"*Then I shall provide you with the proof you need,*" exclaimed Helgi. "Come, Runar, we have much work to do. I swear to you, King Aegir, if any minions of Mortikon or Svaramin are allied against you, I will find the proof you need. Now we must be off to the housing authority to visit Shamuric."

Training

It was drizzling outside when Stefan woke up. The brunt of the rainstorm passed over in the night, leaving sweat from the clouds. Lying on the bed, he covered himself with blankets and stared at the ceiling. *I wonder how Helgi and Father are faring. I've never been to HearthGlen. It might be fun to go just to see the place,* thought Stefan. He was a sight for sore eyes; his arms and legs were covered with welts and bruises, and he had one huge black eye from the training. *Ouch,* as he thought as he touched his right leg. *Those wooden swords really do hurt. I wonder if Rober gets same treatment in the guild—constant training, sparring. Hmmm, I really hope that Rober can come.* A knock on the door broke his daydreaming, and he shouted, "Enter!"

Gjaldakona entered the room along with Stornef, a dwarf; Mikael, an elf; and Smapoly, a gnome. Stornef was a typical dwarf in appearance—small in height but muscularly of build, sporting muttonchop whiskers and a bulbous nose. Mikael was in his twenties—slim, obviously an elf with blue-gray hair, well dressed, and good-looking. Smapoly was, well, a gnome. He spoke with a squeaky voice, was black haired with rosy cheeks, and was attired in typical garb for a mage. "Cackle, cackle. G'day to you, my little one," said Gjaldakona to Stefan. "Let me take a look at that eye of yours." She bent down to examine Stefan's black eye. Stefan shuddered, not from the black eye, but from the big wart on her nose with a strand of black hair sticking out.

"Sorry I jabbed you a bit hard yesterday," said Smapoly in a squeaky voice. "That'll teach ya ta keep yur guard up. Like I always says, best defense is a good offense." Smapoly was grinning from ear to ear toward Stefan. He really liked Stefan despite Stefan's human background. He was totally comfortable around Stefan and had spent some enjoyable times with him.

Mikael, stolid as most elves are, said, "Some of the elven clans from the north have been here and asking questions about us. Gjaldakona spread a rumor in the clan that we were training for joining a band of theives to help with the rebel cause. They seemed to find it an excellent response to keep it a secret but not a secret. Seems to have worked 'cause they stopped asking questions."

Stefan quickly turned toward Mikael. "What kind of questions? Who was asking the questions?" He had a look of concern on his face. "If anyone reveals our plan, then the elven clans are doomed."

Stornef added, "Aye, that was a band of three elves from the north asking about me, Smapoly, and you—where you came from, what we are doing here, typical questions about strangers. Seems like they spoke a lot with Laugalfur."

"I need to keep up my guard up. I intentionally have not told you where we are going or what we are to do. But I alone will decide when and how much to tell you. If one word is breathed of this, we will fail. The race of elves depends on our quest. If we fail, then the fate of the elven clans is sealed," insisted Stefan.

Gjaldakona pointed her scrawny finger toward Smapoly, Mikael, and Stornef and commanded, "Aye, 'tis true. I attest unto ye, the elven peoples will be doomed. I jest not—doomed!"

Stornef bellowed, "I for one am ready for action. I will not fail you, Stefan. As a paladin, I swear an oath to follow you."

Mikael and Smapoly slapped huge grins on their faces and acknowledged that they were a band of brothers; nothing will stand in the way of their tasks that lie ahead.

"Ja ja, time ta do some more training." Smapoly smirked at Stefan.

Runar and Helgi had returned to the rogue guild with good and bad news. Rober was honing his daggers when they came in and was waiting excitedly for the news of the meeting with Shamuric. "Well?"

"The outcome was as I expected—perhaps disappointing to your father, but not unexpected. It seems you have six more months in Blesugrof. There was some anxiety on the part of Shamuric, something about a foreign ruler cannot bestow lands under the sovereign law within the kingdom. When I advised Shamuric that Biggy was not a ruler but a subject, the laws were on our side. When Biggy was crowned as king of the gnomes, it was after the coronation that the land was given down to Agnar and his descendants. At any rate, it seems that your father has bought six months. I do not expect that Blesugrof will survive after this. Shamuric has a typical bureaucratic mind and a vile personality to boot," explained Helgi.

Runar interceded and said, "Aye, Rober, 'tis up to you and Stefan now. I have accepted the verdict. I just hope that something doesn't happen between now and then. Helgi has assured me that he will help in selling the lands at a fair price and not to be seized by the authorities."

Then Helgi surveyed the room and then requested Rober and Runar to accompany him outside. His facial features seemed tense as he put a finger over his lips and gestured to go outside. Helgi whispered, "*Spies, use your stealth mode. When we are safe and unheard, we need to speak.*" Once they were outside and after checking the area to insure privacy, Helgi spoke with a low voice, "Rober, we need your assistance in another task—an important one, if

FORGEMASTERS OF THE REALM

I might add. After you have completed the task with Stefan, I need you too return here as fast as possible. I need you to steal some documents here in HearthGlen. Once you have them, bring the papers to me in the castle here in HearthGlen. And if I may say so, discretion is everything. *No one* is to hear of this, not even Headmaster Able."

Runar added, "And you have my blessing in this matter, my son. They steal from us, now we steal from them. But your primary task must be performed first. Assist Stefan first, then come back and accomplish this one."

Rober's face lit up as soon as he heard the plan. Smirking, he said, "My pleasure!"

2

The Northern Assignment

The weather was dreary and damp, and the sunlight was choked out by the heavy, bloated clouds. Everyone was sitting around the table along with Gjaldakona, drinking flaxen tea. Mikael was inspecting the arrows in his quiver, and Smapoly was simply bored, staring into the fireplace and fidgeting. Stornef was reading a book written in Norsk runes, and Stefan was yawning and stretching. "Sure wish Rober would show up. I'm really tired of waiting. Hurry up and wait, thats I have been doing. I'll be glad when we can do something, anything. At least then we won't be bored," Stefan said to Gjaldakona.

Gjaldkona cackled and responded, "You will soon be wishing you were back here. I promise you that."

"Aye, Stefan, I am agreeing with you. But unless the weather clears up, our journey won't be pleasant. I'm afraid that it will snow later today, hopefully, a light dusting of it. How much provisions do we need? Do we need a mule to carry stuff?" asked Stornef.

"Ah, let me see now . . . about three days' trek to get to the first item. From there, I would guess about three weeks to the next destination, *If* everything goes according to plan. We might have to ration our food, maybe do some hunting or fishing," responded Stefan.

"I needs ta pick some flowers and herbs along the way. I brought me pestle and mortar so's I ken mak'a some mana," squeaked Smapoly.

Cackle, cackle. "I will make extra breads for you. I promise you that it won't go as planned—plenty of hitches along the way, and you will probably have to detour." Gjaldkona cackled. "And once on your way, there is no turning back—no reinforcements, no help, no nothing."

"Aye, we're out for the gold, no turning back," said Stefan. "Say, Stornef, you got any family? I have a brother, Rober, my father, and my mother living in Blesugrof. I don't have a girfriend or anything. We lived too far to visit many people."

Stornef crooked his head and, after a few moments of silence, said, "Aye, me father and mother live in Vokva. Me father don't work now. He was a jewel maker by trade. The humans have destroyed the trade. Now dwarves cannot make a living at it. They can't sell any jewels 'cause the humans cornered the trade. Me sister works in an inn—the biggest inn in the castle. Me girlfriend lives in HearthGlen now, but she might move back to Vokva."

"I've never been to HearthGlen myself," said Stefan. "Is it nice there? I mean, is it a big place—lots of dwarves there?"

"It used to be, but not anymore. I mean, the population of dwarves in HearthGlen is diminishing fast. They used to be friendly. The inns were packed with dwarves and humans too. Now it is a cold place. The humans don't talk with the dwarves. It is like the soul of the city has gone," responded Stornef.

"And you, Mikael? How large is your family?" asked Stefan.

"We elves don't speak of our families. It must be your human half speaking now," retorted Mikael.

"Well, maybe dat's why gnomes like elves so much—few words spoken, but da words speak for demselves. Me, me gots three sisters, all of 'em in Fort Laekur area, 'n dey don't be married either," chided Smapoly. "Ya lookin' to get hitched?"

Stefan laughed and snorted, "Nay, not me!" Then Stefan turned to Gjaldakona and asked about her family. "You ever been married? Had any kids?"

Gjaldakona squinted her eye toward Stefan and said, "Never married. Almost did once. I'll not discuss it with anyone. As for kids, I had a daughter, but she is gone now. Don't know where she is." For a moment, Stefan caught a glimpse of sorrow on her face.

"Whats up with Laugalfur? Why is he so mistrustful toward me? It's like—" Then Stefan stopped in midsentence and grasped his temple with his fingers.

"*Ah, found you again. I need you to ask Gjaldakona to give my old short sword to you. It has magical powers, and you might need it. As for Laugalfur, don't antagonize him. He is a brash and foolish fellow, but he is a natural leader. Your elven clans will need future leaders once we lead them to safety,*" instructed Traikon.

"Aye, I'll tell her. We should set off within a few days," exclaimed Stefan to the invisible Traikon.

Back to Blesugrof

The trio had left HearthGlen heading north. Helgi, Runar, and Rober were anxious to return to Blesugrof to give the news to Björglin. Rober had not been back for more than a year since he had joined the rogue guild in HearthGlen, and he was eager to see his mother again. The trip was uneventful save for the weather, which had started snowing, causing the group to don warmer clothing. Soon the three riders were nearing Blesugrof, and the atmosphere in the air seemed to transform. Rober and Runar were gulping in the freedom of Blesugrof, and their disposition turned to excitement. Helgi remarked that "'Tis good to be back home. I miss having a home for myself."

An hour later, the trio rode up to the main abode: a simple dwelling comprised of thatch roof, rock, and mud. Björglin ran toward the three riders, panting out of breath, as she tried to tell about the visitors. Apparently, five humans had visited Blesugrof and had made threatening remarks yesterday, and she was obviously distraught. Dismounting, Runar told his wife to calm down and explain the incident. After she had composed herself, she explained that the constable from Fort Hermana had told her that if she didn't leave Blesugrof, they couldn't prevent violence. They wanted the land, and that would be taken by any means. "I-I-I don't know what to do. I was all alone here, and they scared me." Björglin was sobbing and confused.

Helgi said, "Let's go inside, and discuss this rationally."

"Mother, we need to take you to a safe place, but where? We can't go to Fort Hermana. The humans there hate us. Aye, let's go inside and try to figure out what to do," stated Rober. Rober was disappointed for not coming back home to a pleasant homecoming, but then, he wasn't terribly upset because he knew that they were being evicted from their home. Needlessly enough, Rober wasn't with all smiles at this moment.

Runar was furious. The local constable was so brazen, which caused him to lose control. "We can't even trust our constabulary. The humans have all but brought war upon us elves. How long do we have to relent to these thieves? How many elves must be imprisoned or killed before we take action in our own hands? I will defend with my life my wife and children! The humans gave us their word—six months—can we not even trust their own words?"

Helgi became angry with Runar and said, "And what will you gain? Killing humans—is that what you want? Nay, verily I say to thee, do not let your anger sway you. We have a plan. Stick with it. You will sacrifice *everything* and gain nothing in return."

Rober added, "Father, we need a plan for what to do next. Is there a neighbor that can give sanctuary for mother—perhaps for a few months—a safe place to live?"

"Aye, we do need a safe place and soon because Blesugrof is all but lost. It might not be right now, but eventually, you need a place to move to. Six months, only six months before the authorities take the land by violence. I suggest that your family should move to Woodbranch in the Sko Forest. At least there you will be safe from harm. I will ensure the elves there do not deny sanctuary," said Helgi. "I cannot make a decision for your family, and I realize the hardship which is imposed upon you. You as a family need to discuss the matter between yourselves. I will leave the room to let you confer amongst yourselves."

Helgi was outside, watching the sunset. With the lack of sunlight, it had gotten cold fast, and he wrapped his wizard's robe tightly around him. He was struggling with the problem in HearthGlen and its change of heart toward the gnomes, dwarves, and elves. They used to be such good allies until the human interferences drove a wedge between them. *How foolish is the human race, all for greed and lust of power,* Helgi thought. *Where do I start looking for the documents King Aegir needs? Who should I start with? Shamuric? Or are there other players involved? Aye, first things first—getting Runar and his family out of harm's way.* Helgi pursed his lips as he contemplated the troubles. Suddenly, Helgi espied a horseman with a horse-drawn wagon coming toward Blesugrof from the direction of Fort Hermana. "RIDERS!" yelled Helgi toward the occupants of the house. Runar and Rober hastily abandoned the abode with their weapons drawn.

A few moments later, Runar sheathed his sword and said, "Strompur! He abandoned his farm and went back to Vokva! It looks like he is bringing his family back." He waved toward Strompur and ran to greet them.

With a "Whoa!" command, the wagon creaked to a stop. Strompur immediately apologized to Runar and said, "Me family has no place to go. Can we rest up a bit afore we have to leave?" Runar obviously saw that the party had been traveling some distance. Strompur was long in face, clearly distraught and in agony, having to beg for mercy.

"Strompur, aye, my home is for you. Make yourself at home, please. And ye can stay as long as ye want." Runar wrapped his arms around Strompur as he hugged the visitors. Clouds of dust were stirred up by the hugging. He greeted one by one the wife and the two children. "Björglin, prepare some food for the guests," Runar shouted toward the house. "And here I want you to greet Helgi the Grey and Rober—you know already."

Helgi pumped the hand that Strompur extended. "Mighty fine handshake—tells a lot of a person. My pleasure to know you," he said. "Did you travel the whole way down here, or did you get any rest?" Helgi was sizing up Strompur. He was chest tall to Helgi, and he had short henna hair. Strompur was barrel-chested and sported huge arms ending with hands that obviously were used for labor. His dark brown eyes had a forlorn look, and he was clearly at wit's ends.

"Nay, we trav'l'd the whole way. No one would spare any rooms at the inns and villages," replied Strompur. He was hectically dusting off his clothes from the hardship from traveling across the lands, and then he tended to his children.

Everyone went inside and busied themselves with making Strompur and his family comfortable. Björglin was making some soup for their famished guests. "Not like old times, eh? I mean, the þorrablot and such," asked Björglin. She thought it must have been difficult for Strompur and his family, especially since they were considered a nuisance. *Strange. I too must be an outsider, a nuisance. I will extend any help I can to assist these people,* thought Björglin.

Anna, Strompur's wife, replied, "Aye, the good times has all disappeared. Here, let me help you peeling onions and potato."

Soon everyone was sitting around the kitchen table with a ladle and scooping the meal into bowls. They were starving as the food was gobbled as fast

FORGEMASTERS OF THE REALM

as they could refill the bowls. The atmosphere in the home had changed from dejected to enjoyable, and soon everyone was laughing and speaking of the good times again. Strompur's two children, two male dwarves aged seven and eight, were soon tucked into their beds. "Maybe we can speak openly now that the children are asleep," uttered Strompur.

"Aye, Strompur, why did you leave Vokva? I mean, these are trying times. Dost ye know that Blesugrof will be gone in six months? Authorities are to blame," declared Runar.

Strompur had a despondent look on his face as he turned to respond to Runar. "Aye, and me don't wanna be a burden on anyone. But the fact is, Vokva is a terrible place now. The humans passed laws that dwarves can only sell our wares to the local authorities at a discount, if ye know what I mean. Tho'ands is now out of work, and the city has fallen in disrepair. 'Tis a curfew there now—only for dwarves, of course—and crime is terrible. Me be's an able-bodied dwarf, and the family said we should leave—better than being a beggar. Now I have heard of a small band o' dwarves in Woodbranch, hoping I could get there."

Helgi and Runar looked at each other, guessing what they were thinking. Rober, with a somber expression upon his face, stated, "We were thinking of exactly the same thing. I want my mother to come to Woodbranch and live there too! Father, please help them. At least we have Blesugrof for a few months, especially 'cause I am leaving. Safety in numbers."

Runar slapped Strompur's back and exclaimed, "Of course, of course. You are most welcome to dwell here. And yes, it is safety in numbers here. And I will not accept no for an answer."

"And not even dream of leaving! I won't hear of it," added Björglin with a raised voice.

Anna fell to her knees, sobbing with relief. "W-we canna offer shekels, 'n' you won't turn us away? B-bless ye, kind people."

Strompur was starting to cry. His eyes were welling up as he had a hard time to speak. "I will na forgets you. W-w-we owe ya more than we have. Never thought me own kind was beholding ta elves. Ya have a friend for life in us."

(Domain P., Pixabay, unknown)

Sko Forest

Rober and Helgi had just skirted Fort Hermana on their way toward Woodbranch. It was almost midday as they neared the Sko Forest, and suddenly, Helgi reined his mount and raised a hand to cease riding. The steeds pranced nervously as there was a *huge* snake in the middle of the road. The snake rose its head, whipping back and fro with its forked tongue darting in and out of its mouth. *"I have not seen you for ssseveral years now, missster Helgi. And who isss this with you?"* greeted the snake. Rober did a somersault off the back of his horse and landed with daggers in hand.

"Aye, Svaramin, we come face-to-face once again," replied Helgi. "You need not disguise yourself. What do you want? What mission brings you before me?"

The snake hissed out, *"Jussst to chat, my old friend."* All of a sudden, the snake was enveloped in a puff of smoke, and when it dissipated, Svaramin stood in the road. "I see you have not changed over the years. 'Tis good to see you again, my friend."

Rober still had his daggers in his hands as he stared dumbfounded at the snake—no, the human. He had heard of Svaramin, mostly from Helgi, but now he finally saw him in person. Svaramin was a thin man, almost gaunt, with long silver hair, and was sporting a long grayish beard. His eyes burned with evil blackness topped with thick, ugly eyebrows. His wizard's robes were white with scrawny fingers and longish fingernails extending from the garb.

"Come now, young lad, you needn't greet me with weapons drawn. You are no match against me. If I had wanted to harm you, you would be dead now," said Svaramin to Rober. "I want to propose an armistice. Let us cease this age-long bickering between us. I want to work together in the new order which the world is now entering," he said to Helgi.

Helgi raised an eyebrow and said, "You mean the new order which accepts only the masters of men? By the way, how is Mortikon?"

Svaramin assumed a pained look on his face. "Can you be civil? I am bringing this proposal in heartfelt open arms. We both know that the world is changing. We both also know that our time on the world is soon to be over. Much like the unicorns and leprechauns, all things pass. The days of matching steel on the battlefield is over. Let us be amicable about this."

"Very well, speak your mind. I at least will hear what you bring to the table," answered Helgi.

"Good, good. What I am proposing is that a city be constructed which is ruled by neither the Northern Realm nor the Southern Realm. It would be a place where ambassadors dwell. All races would be welcome. Let's call it Sanctuary City. The city would not adhere to the laws of the north or south, where any inhabitant or visitor to the city would be expelled for violating the sanctuary. What say ye?" explained Svaramin.

"Nay! Nay, I say unto thee. Like the humans welcome all races? All they want is to make slaves of us elven peoples," shouted Rober, with rage imprinted on his face, to Svaramin.

Svaramin sneered back at Rober. "You insolent pup. The troubles with the elves is of your own making. You meddlesome elves, dwarves, and gnomes have your own thanks for your problems."

"*Enough!* This gets us nowhere. Go back to your master, and tell him that I will consider the proposition. Maybe we will talk later in due course of the matter. Give my regards to Mortikon," stated Helgi.

"Very well," replied Svaramin. He disappeared in a billowing white cloud of smoke.

Rober mounted his steed and spoke up with misgivings toward Helgi. "How could you be so ready to compromise? I thought that you were going to help us elves! How dare you be so cavalier, to say one thing to us and then other things to the enemies?"

"Ah, the voice of youth. I did *not* compromise, nor did I agree to anything. In due time, with age comes wisdom. You will know that what I speak as truths. Svaramin knows, as do I, that we have little time left on this world. His words rang out as truisms. The humans will be the masters of this continent. I, on the other hand, see a future of hope for the elves, dwarves, and gnomes. Perhaps not on this continent, but another. Sanctuary City—perhaps it can work here. But tarry not, let us begin our quest for saving the elves," argued Helgi. He spurred his steed on toward Woodbranch.

Rober and Helgi wandered into Woodbranch and were greeted by Gjaldakona and Laugalfur. Apparently, Gjaldakona had talked to Laugalfur as he was civil as they rode into the elven coven. Stefan and his crew were at her house, preparing to depart, and she motioned Rober aside. Cackle, cackle. She started to say, "How much do you know about where or what we are going to do?"

Rober was revolted by the appearance of Gjaldakona but never let on his repulsive outlook toward her. His eyes never left the ugly wart on her nose with the disgusting thick hair protruding from it. "I know little or nothing at all about what we are going to be doing, madam," exclaimed Rober.

Gjaldakona squinted an eye and cackled and said, "I personally don't think that Stefan has the grit for the job. I may be wrong, but this quest will require some killing, I'm afraid. Look out for your younger brother."

Rober straightened his back and proudly replied, "Aye, I will keep him safe. But I think you are underestimating us, Stefan and me. I don't know where we are going or what I am to do. Can you tell me anything about it?"

Gjaldakona smiled through her crooked teeth and replied, "Only Stefan, Helgi, and me know what to do. Let us go to the house and meet all your teammates to discuss how much you should know at the moment. Spies cannot sabotage the task."

Rober sensed that something was not quite right. Sabotage *is a strange word to use. I think that has a hidden meaning,* thought Rober. "Aye, let us go to the house then."

The reunion with Stefan was heartfelt, and Rober found his companions to be likeable. *Well, a good start, and everyone seems to be agreeable. Mikael, I really like, and Stornef—he looks like he can hold his own in a fight. Smapoly is funny but shrewd,* thought Runar to himself. Everyone was sitting around the table, eating flaxen bread and drinking tea. "Helgi, can you brief us on what we are going to do or where we are going when we take leave?" asked Rober.

Helgi arched his eyebrows and said, "Aye. First, Rober, you should go into stealth mode. Check outside so nobody is within earshot." To that, Rober complied and returned to assure them that no one was around. "First leg of your journey will take you to the Northern Realm, to a blind old man who lives in a cave. But he is terribly powerful, but don't be fooled at his blindness."

Cackle, cackle. Gjaldakona added, "As I hear of him, he is a mage, uses demons as sekhmets, perhaps skeleton warriors or airwharts, and he has a two-headed beast guarding the amulet.[5] Your job, Rober, will be to steal the amulet. You probably will want to kill the old man because if he finds the amulet missing, then all will be for naught as Svaramin will be alerted."

"So that's why you have been so secretive— Northern Realm! Never been there, but I hear it is a terrible place. Also, that is why we can't get help. Everyone there is an enemy," Rober interrupted Gjaldakona with a voice of concern.

Helgi addressed Stefan with "And after you have the amulet in your possession, your brother must return to HearthGlen. I have a job for him there. That means, your party will be without a rogue." Helgi turned to Stornef and said, "Use your healing powers if anyone is injured. By all means necessary, keep the party together. Your last leg of the journey will take you deep into enemy territory. Take the road back toward Fort Hermana, and once you are sure you have not been followed, turn around and go to

---

[5] Airwharts: Demons conjured up in the air as a sekhmet. Sekhmets are guardian pets. They can be tigers, leopards, lions, bears, or demons.

the Northern Realm. Avoid any contact with anyone once you enter the Northern Realm. I will return to HearthGlen after this meeting."

Smapoly gulped and said, "I needs ta make me mage bandages and make more manna too."

As the group finished packing their mule, Helgi strode up toward Stefan and said, "May the gods be with you, and make haste back to HearthGlen, Rober."

The Saga Begins

The group had made its way to the road sign displaying the direction to Fort Hermana. The four adventurers, accompanied by their mules, had stopped for a rest before exiting the roadway heading to the Northern Realm. Rober entered stealth mode to scout for any followers behind. Mikael scouted ahead before them, and Smapoly wandered into the edge of the forest to pick some frost herbs. The wind was biting but not terribly cold as Stornef was looking at the foothills of the Blafjall Mountains. "Four peaks o'er the mountain over there," said Stornef as he pointed in the distance. "Get to the base of the mountain, and then we are in Northern Realm." A slight shiver coursed over him. Stefan knew that this time of the year was winter, and the daylight was dwindling fast. The farther north they traveled, the shorter the days got, and night skies reigned.

Stefan studied the area that Stornef was pointing toward and asked if there were passes or if they had to ascend the peaks. "We can't climb the mountain—the mule. I've never been to Northern Realm, so I don't know the quickest route. Mikael has been there, but I'm not sure if he knows a way around the mountain," corroborated Stefan.

"Aye, me brothers played in the mountains around Vokva when we grew up. Gotta keep an eye open for yeti and wolves," Stornef added.

Soon Mikael, Smapoly, and Rober had rejoined the group and announced that no one was following them. "Well, I guess we should head out. We have about four hours of sunlight left, so let's camp for the night before we enter the Northern Realm," instructed Stefan to the group. As the peaks of Blafjall grew, the weather grew with the mountaintops. It had gotten colder, and the winds had picked up. The intimidation of snow enveloped the group from the skies overhead. The area around the band of adventurers was now totally wilderness. A few deer were spotted in the distance, some wolves, and few birds in the sky. "This will be the last time for a big campfire, so enjoy it, my friends," stated Stefan as the group pitched camp for the night.

Runar was penning up sheep along with Strompur. Leaning on his pitchfork, Runar was taking a break and started talking with Strompur. "What do you think? How is this going to turn out—I mean, the difficulties with the humans? Helgi should drop by any day now on his way back to HearthGlen. I hope that some good comes out of this mess."

Strompur arched an eyebrow, pursed his lips, and replied, "Dunno. I worry about the dwarves in Vokva. I hope no one's gonna do sump'n stupid. What does ye believe? Is there really a land far away? It would be sump'n exciting, being a settler, I guess. Explorer Strompur—kinda sounds good to me. I like the name. I'd like to see me children grow up free." With that, Strompur let out a gruff laughing sound, beaming broadly at Runar.

"I'm kinda worried. About Björglin, I mean. She isn't accepted by humans because of me and the elven clans either. I for one would love to leave these cursed lands, start up fresh someplace else," responded Runar. He hesitated for a moment as if in deep thought and added, "I'm not so worried about Rober and Stefan. Maybe we can try to bring the dwarves back with a new alliance. Gnomes too, I mean. If we don't band together, then we all perish together. Hum, whatcha think?"

"Whoa there, let us not talk about doin' sump'n stupid, getting folk killed and all," cautioned Strompur.

"Well, I don't want to just wait until it is too late. We need a friend like the King of Vokva to stand up and tell the humans *enough is enough*. I'm not talking about killings or anything like that," replied Runar.

"Who, King Bragga? He hasn't got the stomach fer it," said Strompur. He sucked in a breath and continued, "Aye, maybe Helgi kin help to unify us."

"When we went to see King Aegir, he said he would help. But talk is cheap. Let's wait till Helgi gets here and talk about it. Who knows, maybe King Aegir can talk with King Bragga. But deep inside, I know that the solution lies within us, the little people. Helgi can offer assistance and counsel, but in the end . . ." said Runar.

Strompur leaned on his hoe and smiled broadly as he watched his children playing outside. "Aye, freedom—with rich dirt under me to grow stuff, maybe pigs or sheep—'tis me dream."

Strompur, my old friend, we both have the same dream, thought Runar as both of them were enjoying the sight of the children playing. *Not a care in the world, the simple life. Aye, my friend, I have the same dream.*

Svaramin was attending a meeting with Mortikon and his lieutenant, Ormur, in Mortikon's throne room. Mortikon, dressed in his coal-black armor and black boots, was sitting upon his throne made from a block of ice. His head was garbed with a full facial helmet, which only made his appearance more menacing. From the facial slit of the helmet shone eyes like embers as red-hot coals. His arms ended in coal-black gloves rimmed at the wrists by silvery spikes. As Mortikon is a leiche, he portrayed no facial features. Leaning forward upon his broadsword between his legs, he listened wisely while Ormur was speaking.

Ormur, a human who had been a traitor from HearthGlen, had been converted as a loyal Northern Realm soldier by Mortikon. With blond locks to his shoulders, he appeared to be middle-aged, trim, and intelligent speaking. "My liege, the dwarven people are ready to consent to the Althing in HearthGlen. They have agreed to most every demand our contact in HearthGlen has mentioned. As for the gnomes, they will be extinguished forever within the next few years. The elves, however, are a problem. Our propaganda campaign in HearthGlen is working, but because they never really joined the Southern Realm as allies, they are more difficult to work with. And as for that meddlesome fool Helgi—"

Svaramin interrupted and said, "Don't underestimate Helgi the Grey! I have been talking with him about the little peoples and their problems. He seems to be agreeable to having a Sanctuary City, but he has some reservations."

Mortikon jabbed a finger toward Svaramin and said with a firm tone of voice, "And I do not underestimate you. Unlike you, Helgi has defeated us in three wars. It is time to play the humans' hand. Let them destroy each other without any losses from our forces. I tire of you. Leave me. Ormur, I now knight you as Prince Maura. You are to be called by that name from now on."

Svaramin bowed to Mortikon and left the throne room. *I have served you for the centuries, and this is the thanks! Those humans, the vermin that they be—they always will find a way to defeat you. Yes, yes, Sanctuary City* must *be built as it will be the fall of you,* thought Svaramin.

Back in the throne room, Mortikon was agitated as Prince Maura could tell from his voice. "Svaramin has been a loyal vassal, but I tire of him. We need Helgi, willingly or not, to convince the humans to take part in Sanctuary City. I have an eternity to put in play my plans, to impose my will upon them. We can always dispose of Helgi and Svaramin after the city is built. It will be an easy matter to place men loyal to me on the city council. After all, greed is the weakness of humans. Sanctuary City is the first step to rebuilding my empire," declared Mortikon to Maura.

It was almost midnight when Runar, blunderbuss in hand, was investigating a rapping on his door. Strompur was behind him with ax in hand, dreading that some vigilantes from Fort Hermana were there. Peering through a crack, Runar excitedly opened the door as Helgi had arrived. "Blessed be, my old friend. Has our band of heroes departed from Sko Forest?"

Helgi adjusted his wizard's robe after the long ride here. "Good to you see, Runar, and you too, Strompur. As for our compatriots, they should be entering the Northern Realm or very close to it," replied Helgi.

Strompur, relieved because it wasn't any riders from the fort, smiled at Helgi. "We were discussing you earlier this evening. Our worst fears be 'bout to come true. How *do* you plan to save the elven clans? Worse even yet, how do we ease the problems for the dwarven peoples in Vokva?"

Helgi had a somber look on his face as his eyebrows furled. He hesitated a moment and asked Strompur in a depressed voice, "May I be forthright with you?"

Strompur stammered, "Y-yes, please do."

"The problems in the world are not directed toward the gnomes, the dwarves, or the elves. The world is changing, fast changing for the worse. Can I ask you a question? Do you consider yourself as a proud dwarf Strompur? And you, Runar, do you consider yourself as a proud elf? Don't answer quickly. Think about it," responded Helgi.

With a quizzical look on his face, Strompur stared at Helgi for a few minutes. "O'course I be proud to be a dwarf. Whatcha gettin' at?"

Helgi turned toward Runar. "Aye, I'm an elf. But proud of it? Nay. The clans have shunned me because of my wife."

"I don't mean proud because of heritage. I mean are you *proud to be* a dwarf? At least you are honest, Runar. I ask again, do you take pride in the fact that you are an elf?" interrogated Helgi.

"We, Rober and I, talked with Svaramin at the entrance of Sko Forest. I have thought long and hard about what we were discussing. Hold on, I'll tell you everything." Helgi waved off an interruption from Strompur. "Like I said, I agreed with what Svaramin had talked about. I know that my role in this world—and Svaramins too—will come to a close. The ages of the Referees will soon be a thing of the past. All things must come to an end. The problems of the little peoples and the humans too are self-inflicted. The ages of the monarchy are soon to pass. The humans recognized it and created bureaucratic conventions. The subjects of each monarchy had begun to decay from within. The kings of old served as the protectors of their subjects. They worked for for justice, fairness, and for the defense of the realms. Now, the kings are useful for themselves. Greed and corruption is everywhere. I got mine, you go and get your own, so to speak. The humans recognized that. Unfortunately for the gnomes, dwarves, and elves, they have not recognized it. As long as the leaders—and I mean *real leadership*—do not exhibit leadership, then they will be the pawns of the humans."

Both Strompur and Runar were stunned at what they were hearing. The two were staring at each other. Neither one spoke.

Runar stammered out a question, "D-does that mean you're n-not going to help us anymore?"

"Nay, verily I say unto thee. I am chosen by the gods to be a Referee. I *must* fulfill my bond with the gods. What I am saying is that *you* must become proud to be a dwarf or elf, to work for your races. If King Bragga cannot or will not be the defender of his vassals, then you must stand up and do the right thing. The same goes for you, Runar. When have you ever defended your own grandfather, Agnar? I knew him well, and he has been misaligned by the elven clans. He knew that the re-forging of Mjolnir was a duty to his own countrymen and the world. What have you done for the clans—not for yourselves but for your own clans?" Helgi grilled the two

Both Strompur and Runar hung their heads low as they both knew that what Helgi said was true.

"Aye, 'tis right ta speaks honestly. I am ashamed, stewing in me own broth. I was sayin' woe be me too much," stated Strompur with a humble voice.

Runar nodded his head in agreement. "Aye, ye speak as one who is wise beyond the pale. Maybe after you come back from HearthGlen, we should pack up and move to Woodbranch, work at being a true elf again."

Strompur, bolstered by the words of Runar, exclaimed, "Aye, pack up me family to Woodbranch 'n' help the dwarves in Vokva. They deeply need the help 'n' maybe get some hope for the future."

"I am saddened by the events of recent. I didn't mean to scold you or belittle you. Sometimes, a fresh slap in the face to wake you from the trance was what you needed," advised Helgi.

The three in the kitchen were interrupted by a *caw-caw* followed by a rapping on the window. The sound of wings flapping was trailed by a *caw-caw* noise, then a rap-rap-rap sound at the window. Helgi opened the window, and a black crow flew into the room. "What the—" exclaimed Runar.

"Ah, my old adversary, my friend. What news do you bring tonight?" greeted Helgi to Svaramin.

With that, the crow disappeared into a white cloud of smoke and was replaced by Svaramin.

The Northern Realm

The intrepid band of heroes had crossed the boundary between the Northern and the Southern Realm. The difference between the two realms was surreal. Apparently, the Northern Realm was sparsely populated except for animals, but mostly, it was wilderness. The trees were abundantly overgrown in pine trees with a few outcroppings of maples and apple trees. The farther north the group traveled, the colder it got with more wind gusts and snow—lots of snow. The branches glistened as the trees gave off a feeling of coziness as if they were wrapped in blankets of snow. The animal life was abundant here as many deer, rabbits, foxes, and birds in the sky were observed. The skies overhead were laden with clouds, which were trying to peek between the treetops. The group stayed silent as they trudged northward, occasionally climbing a fallen tree in their path. Every now and then were the sound of *caw-caw* from ravens and the occasional howling of wolves. Off to the northeast lay the coven of the dark elves, which the four of them were trying to avoid. To the west were the peaks of Blafjall Mountains, their frost line clearly visible from the distance. Deeper and deeper, the group wormed north as the thick, wooded timberland made travel difficult.

Be dark soon. We need to think of setting up a camp soon. Don't want to get lost in the darkness, thought Stefan. Stefan checked out his companions to ensure that the group stayed together. Smapoly was lagging behind the group as he had to lead the mule around obstacles. "Let's find a good place to camp for the eve. Not too close to the tree line—don't want to be caught up in an avalanche from the mountains. Besides, there is less chance of running into a yeti," Stefan commanded the group. Stornef and Mikael showed their approval of the idea as Stefan waited for Smapoly to catch up with the group. "Rober, can you and Mikael scout around for a good spot near a stream?"

Soon the clan of adventurers was settled around the camp, enjoying a pipe smoke of tobacco. They built a small campfire near a huge snowdrift in case they had to douse the fire in a hurry. Stefan took first watch for the night, then Stornef, followed by Mikael. While they were eating wild oats rolled in honey, Stefan asked Mikael if he had ever been so far north through the woods. "Nay, I have never been this far from the dark elven coven. But I heard tales from the others. I suppose that a pass through the mountains is up ahead, maybe two peaks further. But the elves dared not trespass there. Huge spiders are everywhere there, not to mention the occasional orc, yeti, and wolves."

A *whooo* caused the group to worry as the sunset brought all kinds of creatures out. Smapoly piped up with fear in his voice, "Sounds like the owls are about tonight. Maybe ya better be 'fraid if you *don't* hear 'em," as he searched about in the darkness.

Stefan nodded toward Smapoly in agreement. "I've never seen an orc myself. I mean, I've seen pictures of 'em. Are they terrible like in the stories I heard?" he said to Mikael.

Mikael thought for a moment then replied, "Well, I've never seen 'em close up. They came to the coven to trade a few times. I never saw them as unfriendly or threatening. I guess they are about the same size as humans but with greenish skin with kinda like warts on 'em. They do have some really ugly teeth though, two huge fangs protruding from their lower jaws—fearsome to look at though. The women are really arse ugly, if you ask me. They sport little knobbles on their head for hair—green too. I wouldn't want to take one of 'em for a dance, I can tell you that!"

Stornef snorted laughter at Mikael's remark. "Used to be a lot of 'em round Jarnsmiða afore the end of the war. But they be kinda scarce. I mean them orcs, they been killed off mostly. Now ya gotta watch out for the yeti up there nowadays. Good price for their pelts though."

Smapoly added, "And the yeti fat gets a fair price too, used for makin' health potions."

"Well, I got to stand my watch now. Get you guys get some rest. Stornef, I'll wake you up 'bout midnight," said Stefan.

In the morning, just before dawn, Stefan awoke with a stretch. Looking around to reorient himself with his surroundings, he saw Smapoly busily making more potions. Stornef was snoring as a bull moose, deep asleep. Rober walked toward Stefan and started talking about Helgi, their father, and their mother.

"I worry that once I leave here, you will be without me. Gjaldakona told me to take good care of you," said Rober. "Being your older brother, I want you back home safe. Uncertainty fears me the most, I guess. Just exactly how are we going to save the elven clans? Or the dwarves or the gnomes for that matter too?"

"Dunno, but from what I heard from Gjaldakona and Helgi, Traikon will do something. I guess sometimes in the world, you need to have hope and belief in others," said Stefan. After a few minutes, he stirred Stornef awake with "Get up. We need to get going."

It wasn't very long before the group broke camp and continued their journey northward. They were clinging to the mountain's tree line as the winds from the peak tops washed downward. It was a cold, clinging, damp wind that was wailing with each gust of wind. Off in the distance, they could see the bands of snow falling from the direction they were headed.

The band was startled by the noise of a boulder striking a tree, knocking it down and uprooting it.

Suddenly, the whooshing sounds came from the same area. *"Avalanche!" shouted the group as one* as the ground shook and the forest was swayed by the force of the waves of snow. They ran back to where they were going from to escape the cascading flow as trees were uprooted and boulders bounced downward. It only lasted a minute or two until silence descended upon the trekkers. It took several minutes for the air to clear so that they could see how much damage had been done. "Good thing we weren't camping when it hit. Maybe we should camp further into the woods tonight, away from the mountain," said Rober.

The team of explorers held to the course they had planned and detoured over the massive snow and fallen trees. A few hours later, the stream was at the foot of a huge waterfall, cascading down from the mountain peaks. Stornef was mesmerized by the waterfall and had stopped to view the magnificent sight. "Aye, a sight 'o sore eyes be that, lots o' 'em behind Jarnsmiða," remarked Stornef. Off to the right by several hundred meters was a *hnoðri* indicating which direction was toward Bleakness.[6] As they were investigating the *hnoðri*, Stefan's short sword started to give off a low humming sound—the warning of impending peril. Stefan quickly unsheathed his sword

---

6   Hnoðri: A mound of stones constructed to show travelers the direction of the way toward a town or village. Sometimes, they have provisions for travelers hidden inside for those lost in travels, which are common in Iceland.

and silently gestured to the others. Rober went into his stealth mode with daggers in hand, and Stornef found his dwarven ax ready for action. Mikael leaped into a tree nearby and poised on a branch with his bow ready. Smapoly grabbed the mule by his reigns in case it jolted away.

At a distance of ten meters, standing and staring at Stefan, was a goblin! He wasn't armed, and he didn't seem to be threatening to the group, but Stefan was dumbfounded. He hadn't ever seen a goblin, and at first, all he could do was to stare at it. When Stornef neared Stefan, the goblin broke into a smile and began hopping up and down with arms waving. "Fadur, fadur!" hollered the goblin. With uncertainty, the group could only stand and stare at the goblin. It wasn't a very tall creature, wasn't armed with any weapon, and seemed at ease with the team of adventurers. It had an overly large oval head, huge round eyes, a substantial mouth, and was green skinned with sparse thin black hair on its head. His feet were comical. They were huge and disproportionate to his body. "Come, danger," said the goblin as it was pointing to the road path toward Bleakness. Again, the goblin was jumping up and down and excitedly saying, "Fadur, come, danger!" The sword carried by Stefan was still humming even though there wasn't any peril around. "Quickly, danger," the goblin demanded.

Decisively, Stefan motioned the group back to the waterfall and away from the path to Bleakness.

"Fol-low me," the goblin instructed as the humming from the sword abated. The farther that they followed the goblin away from the path, the more the sword stopped its alarm. The skinny goblin seemed to crawl and seemed to use its legs to lope along; using his arms much like poles to steady his gait. The goblin turned his head toward the group and motioned for them to follow. "Quickly, fadur, danger," implored the goblin.

The crew of adventurers followed the goblin as he disappeared behind a wall of water from the waterfall. The sound from the waterfall was deafening as they penetrated the cascading waters. The goblin grabbed Stornef by his arm, and with the other arm, it was pointing to a small area that allowed viewing of the path to Bleakness. On the path was a group of orcan soldiers meandering along the path. They were hideous looking—maybe thirty soldiers—armed to the teeth, sporting various weapons and armor. They, apparently, were unaware that they were being watched by the band from behind the waterfall.

Stefan touched Mikael's arm and motioned deep into the cave behind the waterfall. It was extremely dark in there, damp, cold, and littered with small boulders and rocks. Soon afterward, the goblin, leading Stornef by the hand, directed the group toward the end of the cave. At the end, they found a huge wooden plank bound with thick ropes that found their way upward into the darkness. The goblin pointed to the raft—obviously a lift of some type—and motioned with his arm toward the group as the deafening waterfall silenced all talk. Smapoly shooed the mule onto the plank, followed by Rober and Stornef. Slowly the three and the mule were being inched upward into the shadowy unknown. A few minutes after the elevator descended, the rest of the group was loaded and began to leave the cave floors. The farther the raft ascended the less deafening sounds from the waterfall subsided. At the top were Strompur, Smapoly, Rober, and the mule, which were waiting patiently for unification. Ahead of them were torches set up in the stony walls.

"Finally, the buzzing in me ears 'av stopped," said Stornef. "I 'av not seen a goblin before, not a real one anyways. Vokva had a lot o' 'em after the wars ended. Me thought they died off."

Mikael added, "Aye, we elves have never seen goblins. We heard stories of them, but they were too far to the west."

Stefan addressed the goblin with "T-thank you. What is your name? Here is Rober, Mikael, Smapoly, Stornef," as he pointed to each member by name.

The goblin blinked his huge emerald-colored eyes and said, "Me, Darling. Fadur, come this way. Me no hurt you. Come."

After about thirty minutes of following the granite walls into the mountainside, the group was astounded by the sight before them. Here was a *city*—an occupied city with goblins everywhere!

Svaramin glared at Strompur and Runar with beady dark eyes. "I come not as an enemy. I come willingly to talk terms. I know that you consider me as an enemy, so it would be advisable for you to not threaten me in any way."

"Aye, stow your weapons," commanded Helgi. "I have thought hard and fast about our last conversation. I am agreeable to the Sanctuary City on my terms!"

Svaramin smiled and uttered, "And these terms are?"

"One—that every race must be included. Two—that the city may never be ruled as a pawn for the north or the south. Three—the city council must be switched every two years with elves, dwarves, gnomes, humans, and the various races in the north. They may not be appointed or elected. The council must be switched for every two-year term. Four—each race must be treated fairly, equally, and with dignity. Five—Mortikon *must* sign a document which states that Mortikon *can never be appointed to the city council*," responded Helgi.

Runar jumped up and shouted, "Why do you believe that Mortikon would ever keep his word?"

"Over the ages that I have known Svaramin, he has never lied to me. I trust his word," added Helgi as he held his hand up toward Runar. "One more thing—if any race or alliance will violate the city, all races must declare war upon the aggressors. These are my terms—nonnegotiable."

"Very well, I will give your terms to Mortikon." Svaramin disappeared in a puff of smoke.

"Now, prepare your families. I hasten to HearthGlen, and when I return, you have a lot to do," instructed Helgi.

(Domain P., pixabay, unknown)

3

Political Bickering's

Helgi had traveled throughout the night in the midst of a light dusting of snow. He was now being admitted into the greeting hall of the castle HearthGlen. King Aegir welcomed Helgi with a warm hug as the two caught up with the events of the last few days. Eventually, the two started discussing the Sanctuary City proposal. Helgi said that the proposal was acceptable provided that Mortikon produce the signed agreement. "Who is going to be the emissary for the matter?" asked Aegir.

"Provided that Mortikon has agreed to it, it will be probably Svaramin initially. Then it will be between the Althing and the northern rulers. I'm afraid that both Svaramin and I are in agreement. Once the deal is struck between the Althing, our roles in the deal will be over, perhaps even permanently between the north and south," explained Helgi as a sad look on his face developed.

"Hmph, let us not dwell upon the negative. I hope the idea of using ambassadors will be the solution. I for one do not relish the idea of bureaucratic meddling. We don't need elected officials running the city," responded the king. King Aegir fixed a gaze off in the distance as if to be in deep thought. "Come, let us take for a walk in the garden. I have some news which may be important for our task here in HearthGlen." Obviously the king did not want to discuss the matter where anyone could overhear him.

After they had entered the garden, light snowflakes were dancing amid the trees, then Helgi spoke up, "I assume, Your Majesty, that the matter is about outing the traitors in HearthGlen—Althing, specifically. I fear the worst for the kingdom. It will only be a matter of time before the gnomes' and dwarves' populations will be in open rebellion, not so with the elves, although the elves will defend Sko Forest with force, mind you. We *must* find out what is behind the building of distrust between them and the humans. Somebody is pulling the strings from behind closed doors."

"Aye, right you be. I can be of assistance to you. I too have my spies within HearthGlen. It will cost you some shekels though. I will have you meet my source tonight at midnight at the Crows Inn, if you wish," conveyed the king.

Helgi arched an eyebrow and said, "Crows Inn? Isn't that the one in the poor part of the city where murderers, theives, and cutthroats live, the seedy part of town?"

It was dark inside Crows Inn. The crowd was mostly two or three lads at a table, a few barmaids, and a gruff-looking dwarf working behind the bar. Helgi ordered a mug of ale and found a cozy nest at a table in the darkest corner of Crows Inn, where he could observe and see who was coming and going. Between the laughter and the muzzled words by the patrons, not much was happening inside. The furnishings were in need of repair, the walls were sparsely decorated, and the floors needed to be swept—a typical lowbrow type of tavern in the poor section of town. It wasn't very long when a hooded, darkened figure had entered the pub. His head swiveled to the right and to the left as if looking for someone before he approached the barkeep and ordered an ale. He apparently had engaged the barkeep in conversation as the character stood at the bar, sipping on his mug. Every now and then, the stranger would look around and resume his posture at the bar. *Hmmm, from the looks of his clothing, he wasn't a thuggish type from this part of the city,* observed Helgi. Suddenly, the barkeep nodded toward Helgi without looking directly at Helgi, and the stranger seemed to concur with something the barkeep was saying. The mysterious stranger, with mug in hand, meandered toward Helgi.

"You are Helgi?" asked the stranger in a female voice.

Helgi was astounded that the spy was a female but didn't let on. "Aye, I'm Helgi the Grey, at your service." Lowering his voice, he whispered, "I have your five hundred shekels as you asked." He cupped a pouch in his hand and pushed it across the table toward her.

"I take that is the total amount? No matter. I will take it at your word. Drink up, and follow me into the kitchen," said the stranger.

Helgi followed the young lady, who was soon in the kitchen, opening a trapdoor on the floor. "In with you. You will need to use this torch." She handed a lit torch to Helgi. She followed, climbing down, and she said, "Keep up with me. The sewers are dark and dangerous here."

The stench was terrible, and the light from the torch pushed waves of rodents ahead. As they sloshed into the ankle-deep waters, the young lady said, "I trust King Aegir. Otherwise, you would have been killed already. Why are you doing this? I know of you, Helgi the Grey, just asI know of Runar and Rober and Stefan. But why?"

"Ah, then you are an elf! I haven't the pleasure, madam," answered Helgi.

"Friða is my name, but you still haven't answered my question," retorted Friða.

"Aye, Friða, I have been helping the elven clans for many years now. If I may—and I may miss my mark—but your mother is Gjaldakona, am I right? I know that she had a daughter, but her whereabouts is unknown," guessed Helgi. "I have been helping the gnomes, dwarves, and elves ever since the Rendering Wars."

"I was told that you were a wise old man, gentle and kind. But the wars of the old are in the past. The new wars are different from them now," admitted Friða. "We *are* engaged at war, hideous and as ugly as war can be, but at war nonetheless. Have you ever wondered what has happened to the gnomes in the city, why they disappeared almost overnight? Ever thought of why fewer and fewer dwarves live here in the city?"

"Aye, Friða, I have heard of these atrocities. They were burnt out, bought out, victims of thievery, thrown in the dungeons, or even the victims of murder," answered Helgi. "I intend to put this nonsense to a rest."

"Well, you are one of the handfuls of humans that even care—that is, if you intend to keep your word," stated Friða.

It wasn't very long before the jaunt through the sewers came to an end. Before them was an old rusted gate built into the wall, and beyond that was the hideout for the outcasts. Entering the den, Helgi was confronted with a myriad of gnomes, dwarves, and elves, and in the midst of them was Laugalfur!

(Domain C. P., unknown)

Goblins and Dwarves

Stornef was astounded as he was staring at a group of perhaps thirty goblins, and in the middle of them was a dwarf! "By the gods! A dwarf . . . h-here?"

"I didn't know that the dwarves even lived in the Northern Realm. Perhaps we *do* have friendly forces to the north! Shouldn't you speak to him?" asked Stefan toward Stornef. "I mean, you are a dwarf."

Smapoly was amazed about the crowd of goblins that had amassed around the mule, sort of like they had never seen a mule before. Most of them were children. He surmised that they were children as he had never met real, live goblins before. They were prodding and laughing at the mule.

As the strange dwarven creature neared, they found he looked like Stornef in appearance. He was perhaps fifty years of age, sporting a flowing long golden beard with gray mixed in, and the beard had been braided down to his stomach. His most predominate feature was his huge hook nose. "G'day, gentlemen," offered the dwarf.

"G'day to you, my countryman," said Stornef in return. "Me name be Stornef. Paladin be me trade. 'N' these be Stefan, Rober, Mikael—all of the elven clans—and this be Smapoly, a gnome."

"Strange group be ye. Why you here? We dunna have many visitors here. Maybe some dark elves, but not any dwarves or gnomes," inquired the strange dwarf.

Stefan interjected with "We are on a quest, a quest to save the elven clans and the dwarves and gnomes from the humans. And may I inquire your name, and why do you live here in the Northern Realm?"

"Forgive me. Where be me manners. We dunna have many visitors. My name be Loftur Jens Loftsson. Forgemaster be me trade," replied Loftur as he bowed graciously. "Me ancestors come from Jarnsmiða and Vokva. Me family moved 'cause the dwarves in Vokva dunna like me darlings, and they be me children."

"Aye, me heard of goblins were there but before me time. Me wondered what happened to 'em," interposed Stornef.

"And now you live here in the mountainside?" asked Rober.

"Aye, best place to be, away from humans and dwarves. Like me said, these be me children, 'n' no one goes afore family," explained Loftur. "Come, come. Let me offer some meal and present me wife 'n' me kids."

The visitors had just finished their dinner and were enjoying a smoke on their pipes. Loftur and his wife were gracious hosts, and they were enjoying the evening, sharing tidbits of news from the Southern Realm and Vokva. Loftur's two sons in their middle twenties and his daughter in the late teens were hammering the group with questions about living in the city. Smapoly was enthralled by the daughter as she was full of life and beaming with jokes and laughter. His wife was capturing Rober in the corner of the living room, not letting him escape from the myriad of questions of clothing styles, city living, and having studied in the guild. Stefan, Mikael, and Stornef were drinking landa and smoking pipes with Loftur.[7]

"So, Loftur, what can you tell me about this wizard in the cave near Bleakness?" asked Stefan.

Loftur exhaled a puff of smoke from his pipe and said, "Ya mean Gamlikarl? He is blind as a bat and mean. He dunna like visitors—keeps to 'imself. Sometimes, he gets company from Bleakness, supplies and stuff from the orcan soldiers." Loftur took another puff on the pipe and continued with "Why ya wanna go there? He won't be friendly, I can tell ya."

"Well, he has something that we need—a key of some sort. I was told that he wouldn't give it up, so we would need to steal it. Do you know the best way to get there?" asked Stefan.

---

[7]   Landa: a strong home-brew whiskey.

Loftur squinted an eye toward Stefan and said, "What kinda key? I know how ta get there. Me darlings raid his garden every summer. But you won't get very far. He uses skeleton warriors ta protect him, and his two-headed pup won't let ya in the place either. Ya canna use Deadman's Pass protected by Orcs, 'n' the Konglos will make quick work of ya."

"Well, how *do* we get there then?" asked Mikael. "If we can't use the pass, then our mule is worthless to us then. The mule can't get over the mountains."

"Aye, right ya be. I'll show you how to get through the mountain. But yer mule still won't do the trick cause o' them Konglos. What kinda key be it? Magic? Whatcha need with the key?" questioned Loftur.

Stefan exchanged looks with Stornef and finally said, "I think we can trust you, but one word of this, and the Northern Realm will wash upon us and the task will be undone. Aye, 'tis a magical key. We need it to open a portal in Vulkanfjall near Joklaberg glacier."

Stornef and Mikael looked questioningly to Stefan as it finally surfaced that the final goal was far in the Northern Realm—*far* within the realm.

"Ah, I see," said Loftur. "Then yer mule won't be of use to you. The *hraunheiða* will lame yer mule.[8] Vulkanfjall—ye 'ava long way to travel, maybe month or so. And the wyverns 'n' wraith riders—ya gotta keep an eye in the skies. I be glad I am not

---

[8] Hraunheiða: Lava fields that have cooled.

goin' with ye. The riders get thick once ya get near Eldfjall."

"Well, how do we get to this Gamlikarl place?" asked Mikael. "I never made it this far west from Sko Forest."

"Me darling Kripling kin show ya the way. Take me mountain goats. They kin carry ya over the mountains. Good be they too 'stead o' yer mule," said Loftur.

The Den

Laugalfur was surprised to see Helgi as if he had been expecting a human from the powers in authority within HearthGlen. "Why did you bring him here?" He pointed toward Helgi and directed the question toward Friða. "Did your mother put you up to this?"

"Nay, I say unto thee. my mother knows nothing of this. Helgi was selected by the king to be of assistance to us," Friða responded sharply.

Helgi looked at the assorted weapons lying on the table and looked upon Laugalfur. "I don't like the implications here. are you going to start something you can never finish? Speak up, and be forthright about it," scolded Helgi as he spoke with Laugalfur.

"What businesses have you here, human? We have a right and duty to defend our peoples," snarled Laugalfur.

Helgi looked around the den and then pointed toward the hundreds of gnomes and dwarves huddled and starving. They were housed in a large room that was damp and mildew ridden, and the occupants were shivering from the cold. "And what with these innocent souls over here? Do they have a right to defend themselves? These poor, wretched persons should be evacuated to a place of safety. The humans won't stop the barbarism against you here. They will hunt all the gnomes, dwarves, and elves until they are exterminated. You can't win. Not this way."

"Aye, Helgi, I know of your plans to save the little people. You see, Traikon is my father, and I know of the Arkaain amulet. We are preparing for insurrection should your plan fail," explained Friða.

"By the gods, if anyone whispers about your plans, then you have doomed the elven clans," said Helgi. "If you have known from the start of Traikon, why were we kept in the dark? You know that I have always been a friend and trusted ally to the elves, yet you played me as a pawn in your hatred for the humans."

"That's exactly why I did not slay you and Stefan on the first day that you came to our coven. You were a trusted friend and ally, but times have changed. We knew that you would not approve of our plan, and we decided to not let you in on it. Tell me now, why should I let you leave here today?" replied Laugalfur.

"You impious fool, Laugalfur. I want nothing to do with this insurrection. That is to say, I will not stand in your way provided," Helgi said, "provided that you allow these innocent persons to leave. I will make arrangements with the king to spirit them away in the night. I suggest that they find refuge in Sko Forest where they can get food, water, and safety. And as for your empty threats, I can have you turned into a toadstool, so spare me the words."

Laugalfur was fuming, but he knew that Helgi the Grey was a master wizard. "Swear to an oath to me that you will not in any way be a hindrance to us. I will take your word as honor as you have always been honest with us."

It was after sunrise when Helgi met with King Aegir in the gardens. "It is worse than I thought, Your Majesty. I fear that killings will sweep upon the realm within the next months. There are hundreds of peasants and needy people in this city. I need five covered wagons to whisk them away under the darkness of the night. Have the city guards manning the gates to let them pass unmolested. I maintain that it is high time to visit the Althing with the proposal for Sanctuary City," advised Helgi.

"Aye, you are a wise counsel, and I will make sure that the wagons leave safely. I will set up an appointment with the Althing after five tomorrow. Will you be ready with Svaramin?" asked the king.

Helgi was occupied with the events of the last few days. *I pray to the gods that our boys succeed because if it fails, the realm will be engaged in revolt,* he thought. The fate of Sanctuary City will be determined with the success of Stefan, Rober, Mikael, and Smapoly. The sniffing out of the traitor will be the least of the realm's problems. *Apparently, both sides of the problem have antagonists as well as saviors. Let us hope the right one becomes victorious.*

"Oh, I was deep in thought. You were saying?" Helgi asked.

"About Svaramin, is he ready to deal with us? Meet me at the Althing after five days, about midday," replied the king.

"Aye, I expect to hear from Svaramin before then," said Helgi.

Helgi retired from the conversation with the king and went to his room in the castle as he was up all night. He was obsessed with the problems with the little people and wanted to dispose of the matter of Sanctuary City. He was starting to feel old and that his time on this earth would be coming to an end soon.

(Domain P., Pixabay 46745, Unknown)

Amulet Taken

The gang of adventurers had chosen their mounts from the flock of mountain goats owned by Loftur. Stefan had to laugh at the sight of his gang perched upon the mountain goats, especially at the sight of Smapoly sitting on curly-horned brown ram, which was bigger than he was Kripling was riding his favorite goat, pulling the supply-laden goat behind. Loftur was giving advice to the hardy band of adventurers, saying, "Cut loose the goats afore ya get to Jarnsmiða. Keep the supply goat till ya gets to the seacoast. There, ya be on yer own. And when ya gets to the peak and go down, don't look down."

Kripling was perched on the lead goat, followed by the supply goat. The rest of the group lined up in a single file behind them as the walls of the cavern were narrowing toward the exit. Ahead, the exit was basking in the sunlight as the skies gave no thought of clouds. The high mountain peaks produced a low moaning sound from the winds, and as they neared the exit, it changed into a low pitch of whistling as the cavern sucked air from the exit.

Shouting to the others, Stefan said, "I am glad to be out in the open air again. This wind kind of ruins it though."

Soon after, the amassed band had found them upon a plateau. The sights of the mountains were astonishing. Snow lay as mother-of-pearl, glistening and changing colors with the sunlight, as the view was gorgeous to the eyes. Interspersed in the snow were a few boulders, which gave off a cold, hard steel look about them, and with the blue heavens as a backdrop, it was as a masterpiece of art. Below them lay the cloud cover like puffs of cotton balls. It was a breathtaking sight, which left everyone—except Kripling because he was used to it—at a loss for words.

"C'mon, guys, come," scolded Kripling.

As the group descended from the plateau, a terrified look fell upon everyone. The ledge they were traversing was no more than a foot across, and one slip spelled instant death. Smapoly paled as he looked down upon the sheer cliffs. "No look down," instructed Kripling. For almost three hours, they descended as they watched several eagles nesting on their perches. The limber goats had to leap across several crevasses, landing onto boulders to safely traverse their way downward. It wasn't long before they had penetrated the cloud line, and it was cold—really cold. The clouds drenched them in dews, and the whipping gales were terrible. Stefan was slapping his arms and legs to prevent his limbs from freezing. The feeling was beginning to quickly lose in them because of the numbing cold. On and on, they trekked toward the ground as it seemed like it would never end. Eventually, they found themselves on level ground at the base of the mountain, and Stefan suggested that they should camp for the night. Nobody complained as they were looking forward to soak up the heat from the campfire and dry their clothes.

Just before sunrise, Stornef was sitting around the campfire and enjoying a smoke as his sentry duty had ended. Stornef wrapped his robe tightly about his body to keep warm. Next to him was Kripling, who was consuming a live fish that he had caught in the stream nearby. "Where be the orcs from the Deadmans Pass?" asked Stornef.

Kripling, with a fish in his mouth, pointed toward the east. After gulping down a mouthful, "Over there," and Kripling took another bite of the fish. Apparently, Kripling wasn't concerned about the Orcan soldiers or that they were so distant from where the band was camping. Stornef gently kicked Rober to wake him, who responded a sleepy "Ugh."

With the receding darkness, Stornef and Rober could make out the landscape surrounding them. It was totally different on this side of the mountain. The lush forests had changed to scrub bushes and dwarven trees, the result from the eruptions from long ago. The flourishing grasses were replaced by mosses and boulders and lava rocks and tundra. "I'll scout out the area. Wake the fellas up. We need to stay on the go," said Rober.

The group dismantled the camp and was on their way. Stefan instructed Kripling to lead the way toward the cave of Gamlikarl. On the way, they saw hundreds of birds that they had never seen before, steam vents from the volcano off to the west, and geysers with hot water shooting into the air from them. It was as though the gang had entered another world. Breathtaking were the sights and sounds. Kripling pointed off to the east as a clearly worn path was visible, which led to the mountain pass and to Bleakness. It was almost a day's trip between the lava-torn landscape and the cave, but they finally arrived. Kripling dismounted his ram far enough away from the cave so as to not be detected. Stefan requested Rober and Mikael to scout the area.

Kripling, Rober, and Mikael crept the way toward the cave, being careful to not be noticed. Rober slid on his stomach upon a huge boulder to scour the area around the cave. Using his looking glass, he noticed six skeleton warriors prancing around the cave. Off to the right, he detected a sheep pen with about a dozen sheep in it. Sweeping to the left, he saw the two-headed dog—a *huge* dog, not a pup as Loftur said. The dog must be taller than Stefan at the shoulder! The dog was sniffing the ground in that area, which was used as a garden. Rober slid back toward Mikael and Kripling and gave them his report.

When the band had regrouped then, they needed a plan. "How are going to do this? The dog is the most worrisome to me. I think we need a distraction, make some way to split the dog away from the skeleton warriors," asked Rober in a low voice.

"Hmm, well, the skeletons would be perfect for using Stornef and Smapoly. I suggest that Rober switch to stealth mode and cut loose the sheep, maybe start a stampede. Can you think of any ideas, Mikael? Maybe I and Mikael could team up on the dog. When Gamlikarl comes out of the cave, you need to be ready because he will surely conjure up some demons," suggested Stefan.

Rober interceded and said, "But you haven't seen the dog. I mean, he is huge. You would have to approach him from downwind. If he smells you, the game is up. And the skeleton warriors are wearing remnants of armors and swords. I can always sap Gamlikarl from behind; maybe backstab him when he starts to conjure up beasts."

"I'll switch to my poisoned arrows then," answered Mikael.

"I can use me freeze spells. Maybe me lava bursts—that would do the trick on 'em skeleton monsters," added Smapoly.

With that, the group split up with Mikael and Stefan taking the dog; Stornef and Smapoly, the skeletons; and Rober after the sheep. Everything went as planned until the wind shifted, to which the dog bolted up at attention and began growling. The dog leapt toward Stefan and began howling with both heads slobbering. The skeleton warriors, alerted by the dog, ran toward the commotion with weapons drawn. Then Rober cut the rope to the sheep pen, and the sheep bolted toward the skeleton warriors and past the entrance of the cave. The skeletons, not very bright, were confused and did not know whether to aid the dog or go after the sheep. It was comical but serious as the skeleton warriors banged into one another in the confusion. The dog, slobbering at the mouths, took to the air in one huge lunge and caught Stefan square in his chest and knocked him to the ground. Stefan's free arm was between one of the jaws and was trying to block the dog's mouths and the deadly paws with his humming sword. Mikael drew his bow and let loose two volleys of poisoned arrows. *Thwump! Thwump! On the mark!* Stefan freed his sword hand, and then he buried it to the hilt in the neck of the rabid beast, causing the dog to whimper in pain. Stornef had charged the groups of skeleton warriors with his ax swinging, causing one of them to dissolve into masses of bone. Smapoly threw three lava bolts, two of which hit the mark, leaving nothing but piles of bones. Gamlikarl cursed out loud. By this time, he had exited his home and was starting to conjure up more demons, and Rober threw his daggers at him. The twirling daggers, containing poisons that Rober made, found the target. *Whoosh*—right into the neck. *Whoosh*—right into the back of Gamlikarl, which caused him to fall on his face. Mikael finished the other skeletons with well-aimed arrows. Stornef ran toward the wrestling dog and Stefan and, with a massive blow of his ax, silenced the creature.

With muffled shouts, Stefan was trying to push aside the dead dog as he was smothered under the mass of fur and meat. Mikael and Stornef managed to drag aside the beast, and they helped Stefan to his feet. With a cry of pain, Stefan yelled, "Oww, my leg! I think my ankle is twisted."

"Lets me see that there, my lad," said Stornef as he helped Stefan to a large boulder. "Yep, looks like ya needs some healin'." Stornef, recited the words of healing and used his healing touch. "Ya be good o' gold in a few. Don't use yer foot for a few minutes."

Rober ran toward where Stefan was sitting to see if he was all right. "I-I saw when you went down. Glad you're all right," said Rober with a look of relief on his face. He went to where the dog was on the ground and retrieved the bloody knife and gave it back to Stefan. "That was close. I was too far away from Gamlikarl when he started conjuring, so I-I threw my daggers."

Smapoly was busy wrapping mage bandages around Stefan's right arm. Kripling came from out of hiding and, with his huge eyes, surveyed the scene.

"Did you get the amulet?" asked Stefan to Rober.

Rober had almost forgotten why they were there, with all the excitement, in addition to this was the first person he had ever killed. With that, Rober and

Kripling ran into the cave, followed by a hobbling Stefan. It took a few seconds for their eyes to adjust to the darkness in the cave, and sitting on a ledge above them was a locked box. Kripling had opened a burlap bag that he had, and he started shoving things of value from the cave. Using his lock picking skills from the guild, Rober opened the box, and within it was the amulet!

As soon as Stefan touched the amulet, it emitted a low hum, and immediately, a ghostly image appeared over them. The image before them was of an aged man dressed with a green shirt, brown pants, and tan leather vest. Everyone was taken aback, and finally, the fuzzy image spoke, "*Ahh, I see you have it. Quickly now, time is of utmost importance. Bring it to me.*"

"T-Traikon?" Stefan asked the figure. "I have never seen you before. Why now?"

"No time. The Scryers will be scanning for me. As long as you can possess the amulet, we can speak face-to-face. I must be leaving," explained Traikon, and with that, the image disappeared.

(Domain P., Volcano black-32829_150, unknown)

4

Fleeing to the North

The covered wagons had entered the Woodbranch coven and had unloaded all their travelers and their possessions. Laugalfur was obviously pleased, as was Gjaldakona. "Too bad that we had to deceive Helgi the Grey, but we needed to take no chances," said Gjaldakona. "He is a good human, as are many others like him, but the lives of our coven are more important."

"Aye, right ye be, madam. I find him interesting to say the least, and as he has proven his word. I find him less of an enemy, perhaps just an acquaintance," replied Laugalfur. "I still won't consider him a friend unless he can convince the humans not to interfere with us, and I do not expect that he will."

Helgi was in his room in castle HearthGlen when Svaramin arrived. In his possession was the document signed and sealed with the stamp of Mortikon. "Should we retire to the gardens? It is a lovely place, and we can speak freely with King Aegir," inquired Helgi to Svaramin.

"Aye, Helgi mine, 'tis a long time since we spoke together civilly. I would be most honored to speak with in pleasant voices again. Tell me something about your king. Is he a dolt or someone to admire?" asked Svaramin. "Not that I am implying that he is feeble; don't take it wrong."

Helgi pondered for a bit and then said, "King Aegir is a fine person, a noble person, and of above intelligence. He is just caught up in the changing world we now live in. He has never been a soldier, nor has he been burdened with war. I'm afraid, with the changes of the realms; he is not of the best of kings. He has never been subjected to the trials and tribulations of the monarchies of the old kingdoms. And, you, how much do you trust Mortikon after we both leave this world?"

Svaramin glazed off in the distance and finally said, "Helgi, I must be forthright with you. Trust—that's not the right word. Trust? No, I do not trust Mortikon. Oh, he will stay in line for a while, but if he has good counsel, he can be kept at an arm's length. But for the fate of the little people depends upon the Sanctuary City—as humankind too—so it must succeed. Should it fail, I fear the worst both for the Northern Realm and the Southern Realm. The last wars were nothing compared to a future conflict."

The three met under a barren apple tree: Helgi, Svaramin, and King Aegir. Helgi handed the document over to the king, which was given to an orderly of the realm. King Aegir found Svaramin charming, intelligent, and a man with honor and dignity. They agreed that on midday of the morrow, everyone will be ready for the birth of a new destiny for the realms.

Helgi and Svaramin had arrived early at the Althing house, an elaborate structure decked out with marble and expensive wood carvings. The king entered and met them at the foyer of the structure and began to show them around. "As you know, the Althing is comprised of two camps: the Framtith party and the Ihalds faction. Your chore will be to convince both camps to support the Sanctuary City—not an easy task as they are always at odds with themselves. I suppose that the Framtith faction wants the realm to reach out into the future, whereas the Ihalds group wants to go slow, think about consequences before they act," explained the king.

"Aye, with the fast-paced world we are living in today, change is inevitable. Not so for so long ago, when kings and queens decided the fates of the realms. It was a simpler life. I suppose that I rather like the simple life myself," said Helgi.

"You will probably be peppered with questions, some of which you can't possibly have an answer to. Just keep a cool head upon your shoulders, answer them when you know them, and decline to speculate when you don't know the answer. You will do all right. After sunset, we have a chance to mingle with the lawmakers in the palace," informed the king.

"'Twas the time of rulers when rulers *ruled*, their decisions were often final. I rather enjoy having the luxury of one-man rule myself, not attending endless council meetings and arguing back and forth," added Svaramin.

Sunset—the orange orb in the sky was starting to go to sleep, and with it, the cold night air left Helgi uneasy. "So what did you think of the meeting this afternoon?" Helgi asked Svaramin.

"Pomp and ceremony is what I called it. I suppose they consider themselves important, brash fools. But this is the world today," answered Svaramin. "But the time will come when the Referees will be at an end. Bureaucrats—I detest them all."

Helgi and Svaramin attended the party hosted by the king. They were introduced to a myriad of lawmakers, some bankers, the head of the constabulary, and clingers of each camp. Helgi found Elmar Lusson, the president of the Althing, to be a strange character. He was a middle-aged man, thin and bedecked in jewelry, and he had a twitch in his neck. Every now and then, he would twitch his head when he was speaking, and Helgi found it annoying.

His introduction to Svaramin and Helgi was rather false. His handshake was like holding a live fish in his hand. Then there was Karl Flakkason—an elderly man, short, stumpy, and dressed with expensive clothing. He was the president of the Ihalds party, and his lisp was noticeable when he spoke. Amid several lawmakers was the president of the realm Banki, owner of the biggest bank in the city. He was dreadful to see, roly-poly with a huge stomach, and a double-chinned middle-aged man. He had been introduced as Penningar Thjova, and Karl Flakkason also presented one Sibbi Ljotmann to Svaramin. Everyone was milling around with a glass of wine and chomping on chicken legs. The constabulary dropped by and introduced himself as Remus Logmansson—a younger man, trim and fit, well dressed, and intelligent.

Overall, both Svaramin and Helgi found the get-together to be boring and tedious, but they smiled graciously and bore the party as best they could. After the party had ended, Svaramin excused himself. "I must report back to Mortikon." And with that, he disappeared in a puff of smoke. Helgi found the king in the hallway and engrossed him with conversation.

"What a crew you have running this Althing." Helgi laughed. "How did we do?"

"Aye, they are a strange lot, but you have to be on guard at all times because they are slippery snakes. You and Svaramin did just fine. Now your part is over. The Althing will determine if or when it will be constructed."

On to the Seacoast

They had the amulet. Phase 1 is now complete, and they would now begin the second leg of their journey. Rober gave his looking glass to Stefan as he wouldn't need it anymore. Stefan concealed the amulet and the looking glass in his knapsack and hugged his brother as Rober and Kripling were departing. "Tell Loftur and all his darlings that he will never know if our quest succeeded or failed. We are deeply indebted to them," said Stefan as the two rode off. "Now we need to close this place up. Hide the bodies of Gamlikarl and the dog in the cave. Best not to tarry as if any orc patrols come by . . ."

After cleaning the grounds as best they could, the group headed west, where the land was hugging the seashore. They wanted to get as far away from the Bleakness as they could. They rode for eight hours nonstop, skirting a few farms, being careful not to be detected. Stefan stopped for a few minutes, scampered upon an outcropping of boulders, and used his looking glass to scour the countryside.

Rejoining the group, he had spotted an ideal place for a campsite, saying, "Looks like a great spot for camping the night, a lava crevasse with a cave. Hold on—to the right, two winged wyverns and their riders. They seem to be going away from us. Best to keep an eye open for wraith riders from now on. Follow me, troops."

They rode for about half an hour, finally reaching the spot. Stefan had Mikael and Smapoly search the cave as he didn't want to be surprised by yetis while he and Stornef took care of hiding the rams for the night. Everyone got comfortable and consumed their cold dinner of flaxen bread and oats rolled in honey. "Looks like Eldfjall volcano is southwest from here, maybe a day's ride. Too bad we couldn't see the Lava Gates. It would be interesting to see it. Anyway, from now on, we need to keep an eye on the skies *and* enemy forces. Yeti is probably thick in these parts—wolves too. No more campfires. We don't want to give away our position," exclaimed Stefan.

Stefan took the first watch for the night, then Stornef, then Smapoly, and then Mikael. It was a cold night, and fortunately, no snow. Overhead, the constant whirring sounds from the *tjorns* soon became normal.[9] The birds were dive-bombing the camp with their whirring sound, but eventually, they gave up as the gang wasn't leaving. Donning his

---

[9]   Tjorn: a swallowlike bird that swoops down and pecks at unsuspecting intruders.

hooded robe, Stefan stationed himself on a large rock for his first watch of the night.

They were nearing the dead winter when the days were getting shorter and the night skies swallowed the daylight. Overhead, Stefan could see the beginning of the northern lights off in the distance. It was an awesome sight, with the night skies shooting colors—reds, blues, and greens—as if the sky were dancing. The lights were racing across the night sky, ever moving like waves of color, never stopping. Stefan was mesmerized by the event but settled down for his nightly duties. *How can such a beautiful event take place in such a bleak environment? At least at this time of the year, we won't have to worry so much about being spotted from above. We can always hold up in a cave during the short d*ay, he thought.

Eventually, Stornef replaced Stefan as the watchman and was given the looking glass. "Keep an eye open for scryers. You'll know them when you see the orb eyes in the sky. Just keep your head down, and don't move if you see one of them. Thank the gods for the dead of winter. They can't see very far," said Stefan.

The group was on the go again after finishing their breakfast. They were planning to skirt the volcano near the North Sea coastline provided that all went according to the plan. "Sun should be rising in another two hours," said Stefan. "Then we need to stop on the hilltops so we can search the area for any enemies. Don't want to take any chances." They could see the top of the volcano as they neared it as the sun was just rising. "I heard that a bunch o' dem orc characters was killed when the volcano blew up. They were inside o' the volcano," volunteered Stornef. They could see the steam wafting off the cool lava, but it still was warm to the touch. Every now and then, the ground would make a belching sound as the little ponds gave off gas from the volcano. The stench of sulfur invaded their nostrils and, with the gusts of wind, made it hard to breathe. Occasionally, the *tjorns* would buzz bomb them when they invaded their territories, and the birds only made them more miserable because of the smell in the air.

The travelers stopped for lunch and to let their mounts rest. Stefan decided after eating his lunch that he wanted to take a look at the landscape and belly-crawled upon a hill. Off to the left and behind them poised the volcano, silent like a statue. Off to the right, by several leagues' distance, appeared to be soldiers riding toward the coast, who were traveling away from the band of adventurers. Not wanting to be detected, Stefan decided that the party should remain where they were until sunset, which was about two hours away. Stefan motioned for Mikael to join him on the hilltop, to which Mikael sidled up the hill to where Stefan was. Mikael took a look through the looking glass, and after a few seconds, he said, "Wyverns—three of them circling around." Scanning toward the coastline, he had observed four or five Scryer eyes in the failing sunlit sky circling the area. "They must be searching for something. *Wait!* Looks like smoke from there."

Stefan grabbed the looking glass and took a look for himself. "Aye, something is burning there. We need to hunker down and get out of here as soon as the sun goes down."

Now it was time to cut loose their mounts except for the supply goat. Stefan instructed everyone to walk for the rest of the journey. He was being true to his word to Loftur. Soon the interlopers were on their way again as it was dark enough to conceal their movements. For five hours, it was slow going because they had to stop often to survey the path before them. At the butt of a hill, Stornef crawled upon the jetty to look. Whispering back to the group, he said, "Take a look at this." Stefan sidled up to Stornef, and he could see the faint orange glow from the distance. He could make out a few bodies on the ground, quite dead. "Seems like ogre peasants or farmers—no soldiers. Seems like a village has been attacked. What do you make of it, Mikael?" whispered Stefan.

Mikael shared the looking glass and swept the area. "Over there! Looks like a column of torches—maybe some soldiers." All of sudden, there appeared two Scryer eyes. "I don't know what to think of what has happened. Almost like farms or villages are being attacked. Why, I don't know. We need to get out of this place, and fast."

"Aye, right ye be. But which way should we go to get around? We can't go towards the soldiers, and we can't go near the village lest any survivors raise the alarm. Any ideas, anyone?" whispered Stefan.

"I kin blink meself t'wards the village. I am small enuf. I kin hide easy enuf. I'll find a way around it," suggested Smapoly.

"Very well. You be careful," agreed Stefan.

Using his blink powers, he teleported himself ten meters toward the village, looked around, then blinked again, and he was gone from sight. Smapoly had never seen an ogre before. They were about the size of an elf with brownish leathery skin and arms dangling to their knees. There were no soldiers in the village, mostly women and children and a few males. It was an agonizing fifteen minutes before Smapoly returned. "Yep, dem be ogre villagers, 'n' some buildings are afire. There be a ravine off the left. We kin crawl around the village," reported Smapoly. He described the village and the dead or dying villagers.

I wonder, maybe they have a problem with little people just as the south has, thought Stefan.

The group, leading the supply mount by its reins, crept along the ravine. For over an hour, they trekked just to get some distance from the burning village. The group walked and crawled as fast as they could safely go, eventually deciding to set camp for the night. Eldfjall Volcano was now a distant memory, and they were within a two-day march to the Cloister Bay. *I'll contact Traikon in the morning; let him know that we are nearing Cloister Bay,* thought Stefan. As always, Stefan was first up for the watch post for the camp.

(Domain P., Pixabay thief man-43511_150, unknown)

Thief in the Night

Rober had just entered the gates of HearthGlen and headed to the castle, where he was to meet Helgi the Grey. He had been riding nonstop since he had left the Northern Realm border, and he couldn't wait to bring the news of the amulet. His journey was slowed a bit from the fresh snows, but other than that, it was an uneventful trip.

Helgi greeted Rober with open arms, and after hearing of the news of the amulet, he had a sense of relief. "Did you have any problems to acquire it?" asked Helgi.

With a look of sadness on his face, Rober told about the fight outside the cave and the killing of Gamlikarl. "I suppose that this will be the first of many of lives that I will take in my journey of life."

"You are getting wiser, my friend, but I am sure that this will not be the last one. We don't have much time to waste, so here is what I need you to do: Target the banker, Penningar Thjova. Be his name, spy upon him, and see if you can search his residence for documents from Elmar Lusson, Karl Flakkason, Sibbi Ljotmann, and Remus Logmansson. I will give you a map of their residences. There may be more people that we have to keep an eye on, but for the time being, let's concentrate on these four," instructed Helgi. "In the meantime, I must be off to Blesugrof. I will be helping your father and mother pack up so they can move to Woodbranch."

Rober waited until late in the evening and crept in the darkness at the bank. Switching to his stealth mode, he scouted around the bank to be sure no one was around. Using his lock picking skills, he found it was easy to gain access to the bank. The uninhabited building looked like any other bank: a teller area surrounded by bars and desks, a waiting area, and the vault area. Rummaging through the desks, he found nothing out of the normal, the same for the teller area. *Guess I'll try the vault now,* thought Rober. As he started to pick the locks, a sudden noise interrupted the lock picking. He heard two muffled voices speaking from the main entrance to the bank. *Click, click.* The sound of the jingling of keys was heard. Rober sat down on one of the tellers' stools and waited.

"Penningar, let's be done with this," said the other man. Now both men were in the bank, and with lit candles, they shut the door and locked it. "Karl, take it easy. Relax. 'Twon't be but a few minutes," said Penningar.

"You know, if it is found out, I'll bring you down with me," said Karl with an implied threat in his voice.

Penningar scowled and said, "Save your threats. If you are found out, I'll kill you myself! Now calm down and we can be done with this. And after tonight, you stay away from me until the coast is clear."

Penningar walked toward the vault and used his key to gain entrance while Karl waited nervously near the entrance door. After a few minutes, Penningar exited the vault, locked it, and strode toward Karl. "Here you go, and you better keep these papers in a safe place," offered Penningar.

Both Penningar and Karl exited and locked the bank as Rober exited from an open window. Rober followed them until Penningar departed. *Now to take a look at those papers!* Karl was walking down the sidewalk when Rober snuck up behind him and, with his sap, landed a *clump* on the back of the head of Karl. Karl instantly fell to the ground, unconscious. Rober rummaged the body of the sleeping Karl and extracted the documents and departed. *Wish I could be here when he wakes up.* Rober laughed. *Now off to Penningar's place.*

Checking the map that Helgi had given him, he crept in the shadow of the buildings until he had arrived. A town crier was yelling to the inhabitants of the buildings, "*Hear ye, hear ye, the midnight is upon us.*" Rober waited until the crier had disappeared down on a side street, and using his lock picks, he entered the house belonging to Penningar. Utilizing his stealth mode, he surveyed around the room. It was an apparent living room of some kind, bedecked in expensive furniture's and paintings. After checking all the rooms on the first floor, Rober climbed the stairs, where he found three closed doors. The first room was a bedroom with an adjoining bathroom, empty. The second room contained Penningar, sound asleep in his luxurious bed. *Here is where he would keep the secret documents probably,* he thought. He looked through the desk, under the bed, behind the chest of drawers, and came up empty-handed. He looked behind the pictures on the wall—nothing. Penningar turned to his side to be comfortable and soon was snoring pleasantly. *Ah, stupid me. Let me look under the rug!* Thought Rober. He lifted the rug, and sure enough, he had found a hidden trapdoor bolted with a lock. He quickly undid the lock, and inside was a myriad of papers and documents. Rober retrieved them, cleaning any evidence of having been there, and left the house. *Now to go back to the castle and savor my treats.*

After Rober went back to his room in the castle, the treasure trove was lying on his bed. Most of the documents were of a personal nature, and some were normal business documents. He segregated from the pile the three that were of interest to him and shoved the documents in a bag. *I'll get rid of these after going back for more,* Rober thought. Turning to the three documents that had interested him, he browsed through them and found that they were ledgers of some type. There were amounts being paid to a company by the name of Resource Planning, but no name was attached. *Guess I'll have to snoop around the housing authority to find out who owns or operates Resource Planning.* It seems that large chunks of land and such around Vokva were the subjects next to the ledger entry and the total amount of one hundred thousand shekels. The next ledger contained names next to the amounts they had received. Well, *what do you know? These are the very ones we were looking for. Elmar Lusson, Karl Flakkason, Sibbi Ljotmann, and Remus Logmansson—crooks, if I ever saw one,* thought Rober. The third ledger was about payment to Master X for the amount of five hundred thousand shekels. *But I still don't know who Master X is and what his connection is.*

Karl Flakkason found himself waking with a "Humph" and sat up, wondering what had happened. He thought he was all right, no injuries or blood as he checked himself out. He was confused for a moment as to why he had suddenly blacked out. He scolded himself for ruining his expensive clothing until he patted himself down, looking for the documents. "*Gone!*" shouted Karl as a panic began to swell within him. "*By the gods, I need to think for a moment. I can't panic now—clear my head. What am I going to do now?*" His beady eyes swept the area where he had fallen with his tongue lipping his lips. Maybe he had dropped it when he fell. Scratching his head with a frightened look upon his face, he searched the area for several minutes but to no avail. *"I'm done in now. I can't call the constabulary. I can't tell Penningar. Oh, woe is me!"* He racked his brain to try to come up with a solution. After a few moments—like a light shone upon him—he smiled and said, *"I know. I'll go to Able. He can help, always been helpful when people are in a jam."*

Karl found himself rapping on the window at the bedroom of the rogue guild. *"Wake up, you fool."* He tapped on the window repeatedly until a lamp was turned on. "It's me," whispered Karl to Able. "I need your help, and I need it fast."

Able, still asleep, composed himself and mumbled, "Just a minute. I'll let you in the back door."

It wasn't very long before both of them were in the guild master's office. "I'm in trouble—big trouble. Some things have disappeared, and I got plenty of money for you," initiated Karl.

"Whoa, slow down. Now what is all this about? What kind of things? And what do you mean you have money? I thought you bureaucrats could fix things," asked Able.

"Well . . . you see . . . uh, I mean . . . you see, I have a . . . problem," replied Karl.

"Spit out, man! Tell me everything," retorted Able with a skeptical look on his face.

After Karl had related the incident to Able, he rubbed his chin and squinted an eye at Karl. "Hmm, sounds like you have a serious problem on your hands. Let me get dressed, and I'll meet you across from Crows Inn. Use the back door, and make sure you aren't followed."

Sounds like the work of a rogue, perhaps a mage, thought Able.

Able spotted Karl under the shadow of the building next to the Crows Inn. "Follow me," he instructed Karl, and they disappeared into an alleyway. All of a sudden, Able spun around and with dagger in hand and buried it to the hilt in Karl's chest.

Abandonment

Before the two families—Runar's and Strompur's—had left Blesugrof, they paused on the hilltop for a moment. Björglin was openly crying, with Anna attempting to console her. Runar had a lump in his throat as he glazed for the last time upon the homestead. Helgi said nothing as there was very little to make a difference. After some minutes, Helgi rode his stallion up to Runar, placed a hand on his shoulder, and said, "I think it is time to leave now," with a sad, solemn voice.

They skirted Fort Hermana and made their way to Woodbranch. As they were entering the coven, Gjaldakona cackled. "Have you heard?" She was nervous and distraught, which was apparent.

"Heard what?" asked Helgi.

"You haven't heard? By the gods, one of the Althing has been assassinated! And Laugalfur and my daughter are trapped in HearthGlen," squalled Gjaldakona, almost breaking out into tears.

Helgi broke into a rage. "I knew this would come to this! I warned Laugalfur and Friða. Now the humans will turn to open violence against the elves. And, you—you are complacent in this. Do me a boon: take good care of Björglin. She needs all the help she can get. Now you will see that I have been right all along. Now nothing good comes from this. NOTHING!" He calmed himself down and commanded, "I will hasten toward HearthGlen to do what I can do. In the meantime, you elves need to round up the courage to listen to Runar. And you, Strompur, fly with the winds to Vokva. I fear it is already too late."

Stefan and his band were getting ready to head out toward Cloister Bay when all of a sudden; the party was peppered with boulders and rocks. A huge yeti was growling obscenities as he was hoisting another boulder over his head. Three other yeti were loping toward the group, slobbering for their next meal. Stefan was already with the humming sword in hand when a huge rock slammed the side of his head, which left him momentarily stunned. Smapoly, quick to act, threw a freeze spell on the yeti getting ready to cast the boulder, which caused him to be suspended in his tracks. The frozen yeti then shattered under the weight of the boulder, crushing him into pieces. Mikael was lobbing arrows at the three yetis while Stornef, with ax in hand, rushed out to meet them. Smapoly switched to lava bursts while Stefan, with blood running down his head, ran out to assail the first yeti. With a leaping, turning motion, the elf took a swipe of his sword, leaving the yeti howling in pain as its arm separated from its body. *Thwump, thwump,* sang the arrows as they found their marks. Stornef's targeted yeti clawed him, but it was only a glancing blow. Stornef hoisted his ax over his head and struck a decisive blow upon the other yeti. The band was surprised by a shrieking and the flapping of winds from above. The wraith rider was investigating the commotion caused by the yetis. Stefan yelled "Wyvern!" as he clamored toward the wraith rider. The smell from the beating wings and screeches was putrid. While Mikael targeted the wyvern, Smapoly cut loose with another freeze spell, and the noises from the battle concerned Stornef. Stefan was parrying the claws from the wyvern, the clanging noises from the humming sword adding to the din to the battle. When the freeze spell found its mark, the bird seemed to be suspended in midair for a second, and then it plummeted to the ground. Stefan took a sidearm swipe at the rider, which left the rider headless.

Stornef ran toward Stefan and used his healing powers as Stefan was asking if everyone was all right. "We need get out of here. There will be more wyverns to find out why it didn't return," commanded Stefan. Smapoly was drinking manna and said, "When we get to a safe place, I needs ta make more potions. I'm low on manna."

The group departed posthaste, keeping an eye on the skies. It was not very long before the sun found its slumber as the darkness fell quickly. For about five hours, the band trudged through the tundra and lava formations and finally decided to rest up and let Smapoly concoct more manna. Stefan retrieved the amulet from his knapsack and confronted Traikon. "We're almost to Cloister Bay. What next?"

"Good, good. Off to the right is the area around Cloister Plinth. You don't want to be anywhere near that place. It is a training academy for mages and wizards. Stay on the way which you are now on. You will see some ogre villages. Steal a boat and go due west till you land on the other side. After that, you need to keep a sharp eye on the mage towers—Scryers. Oh yeah, I forgot to tell you: in the sea, keep away from the icebergs. Not good for boats," advised Traikon.

"Well," said Stefan, "I guess we should cut the goat supply loose pretty soon. I scanned the area in front of us, and I didn't see anything unusual. In another ten hours, we should be on the coastline then search for a boat to steal."

With Smapoly being finished in making more potions, the gang took off toward the coastline. The *tjorns* were still dive-bombing them every time they invaded their nesting areas, and the howls from the wolves were still with them. The landscape was turning to more tundra and less lava, which meant more bogs and slushy traveling. The moon was dipping between more layers of clouds, which probably meant snow. The winds were picking up as they got closer to the shoreline as well as the group stopped to don more clothes. Their breaths were visible in the cold, frigid air, and Stornef was starting to build icicles in his beard. They made some good time considering, and they were finally there. A scan of the shoreline revealed a small ogre fishing village, and Stefan decided to hold up in a cave in the lava crevasse, which was probably a ten-minute trek from the village. "Rest up. I guess this is just about past midnight. Go out and steal the boat and be a-sea after in about three hours before anyone would be out and about."

Rober had secreted the documents in Helgi's room and went after the housing authority building. It was so easy; he had no problem finding out who owned or operated Resource Planning. It was none other than Remus himself! *So while Remus was locking up dwarves and elves, he was stealing their property. Constable my foot! But is Remus Master X?* Rober sped off back to the castle; he had finally found enough proof that most, if not all of them, were crooks, and he wanted the king to dissolve the Althing until they could be arrested. *I better wait in Helgi's room till he comes back. He'll know what to do.*

Lying on the bed to contemplate the next move, Rober heard a commotion in the castle. "To arms! To arms! A member of the Althing has been assassinated! To arms!" a castle guard was screaming. He leaped out of bed, switched to his stealth mode, and ran toward the king's greeting hall. There he found Remus screaming to the king,

"It's those disgusting elves, I tell you! I've warranted for the whole lot of them. I heard from my spies that they were planning something! The den of thieves is surrounded. We're going to take'm dead or alive! Let's revenge the death of Karl."

Rober was stunned. *Karl was murdered? And I bet who was behind that: that disgusting Penningar. But what to do?* He racked his mind and then made a decision. He raced back to the room and scooped up the documents and ran back to the greeting hall. Remus had already left, and the king, with Jon next to him, was silent with his head hanging between his knees. "May the gods be favorable upon us. I fear a revolt, go and fetch a court scribe so we can at least tell our side of this," said the king toward Jon. The king was totally shocked; this was his first real crisis as the king, and he absolutely was at a loss as to what to do. Rober sidled up to the king and whispered, "Psst, it's me, Rober."

The king looked around and found no one. "Psst, it's me, Rober. I have all the documents you required. It seems like the elves are about to take a fall for a murder they didn't commit," said Rober.

"Where in the devil are you?" asked the king.

"I'm in stealth mode. I can't be seen talking to you or anyone from the castle. I'll leave the documents in a bag next to the fountain in the garden. And if it gets ugly, I'll do everything I can to help the elves or the dwarves and the gnomes. I swear by my ancestors," Rober flatly spoke out.

The king stood up and ran toward the garden area. Hidden next to the fountain was the bag of documents, to which he swept the bag up and returned to the throne area. His face turned red as he read one after another of the documents. He was furious and at a loss as to how to respond to the news. The court scribe entered the throne area along with Jon, and the king immediately dismissed the scribe, saying, "Jon, we have a crisis upon our hands, and I need the best counsel you can give me. Dismiss the scribe, but don't let him go very far. I need to take an action as any real king in before my time. I want every detail written down."

Stefan had already turned the lone goat loose, so everyone had to carry their own load of supplies. Stefan and his group crept down to the shoreline, constantly with eyes open for any motions to indicate that a villager may be out for a stroll. Smapoly nearly leaped out of his skin when a Tjorn suddenly dive-bombed the group and made a whirring sound. Ahead was a rowboat beached in the sand, and it looked like it would do to get across the seas. Stefan used his looking glass to scan the area and found nothing unusual. He instructed Smapoly to blink into the boat and make sure that the oars were there as well as the anchor, to which Smapoly complied. Smapoly returned to the group and whispered that it was good to go. Everyone except for Stefan and Stornef loaded their supplies into the boat and boarded while Stornef and Stefan pushed the boat into deeper water. With a finger over his lips, Stefan began to oar. Slowly but surely, the boat made some distance where they could speak in normal tones.

The skies had started to spew sleet, and the waves were getting bigger. Soon they were rowing as fast as possible just to keep up a forward movement. Every now and then, a crack, a crash, a boom, and a splashing noise were heard when the glacier gave birth to huge chunks, which fell into the ocean and formed icebergs. Occasionally, some of the icebergs floated behind the rowboat, which actually pushed the boat farther along their path. No one was speaking in the rowboat. The howling winds made hearing difficult. Stornef manned the oars to give Stefan some rest from the constant pumping and pulling on the oars. Everyone was soaked from the splashing of the waves, and they were left with a salty crust on their clothes.

The dawn this far north was spectacular to see. Intermittently, the group would catch a glimpse of a pack of seals as they hitchhiked on the ice floes. They rowed on for what seemed like an eternity, but it was actually for about five hours as they could catch of the glimpse of the shoreline. The seagulls were aloft, wafting in the air currents over the gang's heads. '*Soon. Not far to go now*', thought Stornef.

Perilous Outcomes

Strompur was just entering the main gate of the castle Vokva when he noticed a crowd around the bureau of dwarven affairs. Standing outside the bureau was the chief of the office, one who called himself Gisli Vorkennasson. He was scolding the group, comprising some thirty or forty dwarves, and was commanding them to return to their homes. "Now look here, you are making a bad name of you dwarves. Don't make us take action against all of the dwarves. Now scat. Run off home. We will distribute some provisions when you act as law-abiding citizens."

Strompur tapped on the shoulder of one of the dwarves in the crowd and asked what was this all about. "Aye, they donna wanna give us stuff, blankets 'n' food 'n' stuff. HearthGlen says now we be under curfew. Us dwarves, I mean." Strompur looked around the crowd with dismay. These inhabitants were starving. And in the middle of the winter, they needed blankets, coal for heating their homes, and food for their children. Strompur, not wanting to stand for it anymore, went into a fit of rage; he ran to the head of the crowd and stuck his arms over his head. Yelling at the top of his lungs, he broke into a sermon for the dwarves. "Look at'cha. 'N' you call yourselves dwarves? We donna want anything from these disgusting humans." He pointed a finger toward Gisli. "Why don'cha stand up 'n' be a proud dwarf, not a pet dog when HearthGlen throws foods to the floor? We used to be proud, hardworking, takin' care'a our families and children. Now whatcha become? We used ta be a mighty realm, ne'r were sorry for being a dwarf! Well, I say enuf is enuf. Swallow yer pity, roar as a lion—as proud 'n' majestic—and I say nay ta this Gisli fool 'n' his band of cutthroats in HearthGlen!"

The crowd yelled approval of Strompur as the gathering got louder, attracting many more dwarves from passersby. Gisli, with fear and anger, said to Strompur, "I'll have you in the stocks, you insolent, disgusting dwarf." He motioned for his bodyguard to take Strompur into custody, to which Strompur cut loose with an uppercut straight to the chin of the guard. The guard fell immediately to the ground, knocked out cold. Gisli ran into the office and bolted the door.

The crowd cheered, threw their hands into the air, and screeched their approval. "Let's break down the door, take what we needs. No more begging from us!" shouted Strompur. The door creaked and groaned under the weight of the assailants and finally gave way. By now, the crowd had become a mob, attracting more participants; some were bringing lit torches and weapons. Not wanting the mob to be out of control, he began commanding the ones near the door. "No killings! No KILLINGS! Donna burns down anything. We only want what is due to us. Take Gisli alive. You there, getcha tar and feathers. I want him tarred and feathered 'n' sent back to where he came from." Strompur felt like a new person—that he could control the crowd—and they loved it. He never in his life thought that he was in control, but here he was, the leader of the throng of dwarves. *I'm in control. For once in many years, I have control over me life.* Strompur smiled. *These dwarves need leadership. Leadership. Strompur, donna fail me now. Dey needs me.* With the idea firmly in his head, Strompur started directing individual dwarves and assigning different tasks, ordering others to help in unloading the supplies from the office. He knew that soon, the royal guards would break up the group, perhaps to arrest some of them. He wanted to be ahead on their plan of action, so he grabbed about thirty dwarves who were loitering around and marched them down the street toward the castle. "The guards will prob'ly come from dis direction." He pointed a finger toward the castle. "Whatever you do, donna obey any commands, 'n' if you have to, defend yourselves. We've come too far to turn back now."

King Bragga was beside himself. He looked confused and unable to make a decision. He knew of the assassination in HearthGlen, knew that the real reason for the curfew was the killing. The only problem was, he never announced it to the populace. From the balcony attached to the king's bedroom, he watched as the peons in Vokva were almost in total revolt. It must be that half of the inhabitants of the city were involved. "Send out the guards. No, wait, maybe I should address the citizenry. I don't know what to do. Germaine, do something. You're my counsel!"

Germaine, his loyal royal counsel, put up his arms and just shook head but said nothing for a moment. "If this gets out of hand, maybe you should flee the city. Perhaps HearthGlen will take you in. Maybe they'll have pity on you for all the years you have assisted the humans."

King Bragga watched from above in his balcony as the mob dragged Gisli bound hand and foot toward the main gate. King Bragga was wringing his hands, and fear washed upon his face; he had never seen an actual tarring and feathering, and he shuddered as he didn't want to be next. The sounds from the mob were terrifying—all the screaming and shouting, making demands and threats. "Over there! Looks like the leader of the revolt. Maybe I should invite him to the castle, make some concessions or something."

Strompur was awaiting an assault by the royal guards, but to his surprise, it never happened. "What the devil are dey be up to?" said Strompur to the posse surrounding him. "Why haven't the royal guards been dispatched?" The group began to fidget. The response from the castle was, well, nothing. Finally, Strompur addressed the group and, trying to reconcile the mob, said that they should march toward the castle. "If dey wonna come to us, then we will come to dem!"

With that, the multitude began to march to the castle.

Before the masses had reached another hundred meters in their march to the castle, the king appeared on the balcony. "Citizens of Vokva, desist and stay your assault upon the castle. I, King Bragga, wish to speak with the leader of this pack of dwarves." The crowd stopped and stared at the king. "We can work out our problems peacefully. I beseech the leader of this crowd to come forth and speak with me."

Strompur shouted back, "And if this is a trap? I am willing to speak with you, but I warn you, if this is a trap, I'll have the castle razed to the ground!"

"This is no trap. I'll send out one of the royal guards to escort you inside," insisted the king.

Helgi had made in record time his journey to HearthGlen. On the way here, he had witnessed the massive crowd of humans thronging in Fort Hermana. Blesugrof had been put to the torch as well. He was stone-faced and was in no mood for any protocol. Racing into the throne room, he demanded to be in the know about what had happened. Rober ran into the room after Helgi had entered and whispered,

"Karl is dead, and I think Penningar was behind it. Now they want to hold all little people responsible!"

King Aegir had aged overnight; ever since the murder, he knew that the kingdom was in dire straits. His fear was that of the vigilantes. Someone would do something to make the matters worse. The problem for the king, however, was that Althing had bound his hands in the matter. Remus and many prominent members of the Althing were agitating the ordinary citizens, demanding all dwarves, gnomes, and elves be held responsible. "Helgi, I hold myself responsible for many things, but I am powerless. I have read the documents as you acquired for me. But I don't have the authority to do—" All of a sudden, there was a rustling sound that came from behind the curtain behind the throne. A dagger was flying through the air, landing in the chest of Helgi. Helgi broke out a whimper as the weapon landed with a thump. Helgi fell to the floor with his robes drenched in blood from the wound.

The king leapt from the throne to assist Helgi while Rober rushed toward the rustling curtains. "Guards! Guards! Guards!" shouted the king. But it was too late. The king held Helgi's head in his lap with the king's tears flowing. "Why? Why? Who could have done such a thing?"

Helgi, struggling to speak, said, "B-be a . . . a king. W-w-we ne-need a king . . ." The king could do nothing to help as he watched the life dissipate from Helgi's body.

Rober ran back into the throne room to report that the culprit had arrived. He stopped in his tracks, shocked, to find Helgi died. In a fit of rage, Rober shouted at the king, "All this was because he was trying to help our little people! Have you no shame? Where is your honor? Where is your chivalry? Be a king, *A real king*, instead of making excuses. As for me, I am now considering myself an enemy of the kingdom!" Tears were flowing down his cheeks as he wiped them from his eyes.

A royal guard suddenly ran into the room and announced that Remus and his posse had taken Laugalfur and Friða into custody. Rober went into his stealth mode as he said, "You are responsible. I am now an enemy," and he fled the room, undetected.

Svaramin felt a horrendous pain his chest as he fell to his knees, clutching his chest, and he emitted a sobbing cry. He knew then that something horrible had happened, and he felt a sorrow as one in his heart like one who had lost a loved one. Deep inside, he knew that Helgi the Grey was now gone, that the Referees were now at a close as the exit doors were being closed in the bins of history. He knew also that his course in history will soon come to an end. *Time to call upon Prince Maura and Mortikon,* thought Svaramin.

Prince Maura and Mortikon were in the throne room of Mortikon. Mortikon was discussing who gave the order to kill Helgi the Grey. He was not pleased and was not in a mood for idle chat. "Did you give the order to kill Helgi? If not, what do you know of the killing?" asked Mortikon.

"Nay, sire, I did not order the killing. It seems that one of our agents in HearthGlen took it upon himself," answered the prince.

"Then find out who and why, and execute him. Now!" commanded Mortikon.

Then with no advance notice, Svaramin appeared before them, wanting some answers from the two in front of him. "We were just discussing matters concerning Helgi the Grey and yourself. My condolences for your loss," said Mortikon.

"My loss? My loss? What do you think have you done? You have set back the progress towards Sanctuary City. How about *our* loss? Both of you are fools. Now the Referees are finished. How dare you to talk about my loss!" screamed Svaramin, obviously enraged.

Mortikon was clearly irate at the tone of voice used by Svaramin. "Hold your tongue, you worthless wizard. I was investigating the killing, and I am ordering the prince to hold the killer responsible, you dolt!"

"He was killed on your orders. Don't deny it. He was the enemy, but he was of the same coin, only the other side. You, by your bumbling, have destroyed everything!" shrieked Svaramin.

"I've had enough of you and your incompetence. I'll have nothing further to do with you, Svaramin," Mortikon said, and with that, his eyes began to glow a deep red color, blasting a bolt toward Svaramin.

Svaramin disappeared before the bolt could reach him, and from the air came a voice, saying, "Very well, our pact with the gods is finished. Did you really think I would be stupid enough to have appeared here in person? The gods will have the last word of this matter," and Svaramin left the castle.

5

Traikon Delivered

The assemblage was now back on land, and they needed to find cover before the dawn's lights revealed their presence. Stefan was already scanning the enormous cliff walls before them. It was difficult to spot due to the poor light in the darkness, but he had found what appeared to be a cave just up ahead. "We'll have to scale the cliff, maybe half-way to the top. Looks like a perfect spot to pitch camp inside of it. Mikael, find some driftwood or lumber on the shoreline. I'd like to feel some heat from a fire myself. Smapoly, see if you can blink up into the cave. Check out if anything is in there." Smapoly complied with the request as Mikael commenced with his task. Soon, with the firewood damp but usable and the cave found to be uninhabited, the company of adventurers, after a lengthy climb, had reached their goal. Stornef was busy with making the fire as

Stefan cautioned him not to make a huge fire. Mikael had found some *Lundi* eggs, which was a treat.[10] Soon they were cozy and sated from the eggs and the warm glow of the fire.

With the sunlight above and the cave masking their campfire, there was little chance of being detected. Stefan told the group to take a rest and that he would be the camp guard. "I need to contact Traikon anyway," he asserted. "As soon as the sun sets in about three hours, we can scale the rest of the way to the top. We should be at Vulkanfjall within two days or so." The rest of the unit slept while Stefan postured himself before a boulder and commenced his duties as guard.

The sun was dipping below the horizon when Stefan retrieved the amulet and contacted Traikon. "Well," said Stefan to the ghostly figure, "we have made ashore. We should be there in about two days or so."

"Good. Be ever watchful for Scryer eyes. Did you hide the boat? You—wait—Scryer! He has detected the magic from the amulet!" Suddenly, the figure disappeared. "How stupid of me, not hiding the boat. Get up, fellas," shouted Stefan. He kicked Smapoly on the leg and punched Stornef. "We've been detected. Douse the fire, and quickly go to the back of the cave, the darkest corner. Make haste. The Scryers will soon be all over us!"

---

[10] Lundi: a bird commonplace in Iceland (puffin bird), which are a delicacy, as are their eggs.

It was not five minutes before the Scryer eyes were combing the shoreline. One of the eyes had stopped and was hovering over the rowboat, turning in all directions to detect the intruders. "Won't be long now afore they search the cliffs! We dare not leave the cave, and there is too much light in the sky. They would spot us instantly, and the game would be up," whispered Stefan to the gathering. True to the words, an eye appeared and had been trying to peer into the cave. Hiding behind fallen boulders and rocks, the band was hoping that the eye would leave without detecting them. *Please don't detect the campfire smoke,* thought Stefan anxiously. Apparently, they were not detected, and the eye left the area and concentrated on the shoreline. "What do we do now? We can't leave the cave yet, too much light outside for about an hour or so," whispered Stornef.

"We'll wait it out," responded Stefan. After about a twenty-minute wait, Stefan crept to the entrance of the cave. Dismayed, he spotted a *Karvi* manned by five Orcs and a human mage.[11] He rejoined the group and related his findings. "If they land, then they will surely find us. Let's take out the mage first. He can alert other mages besides conjuring another eye. We can probably take out the orcs as they have to climb up to get us. Mikael, arrow your bow up. Smapoly,

---

[11]   Karvi: A longboat used by the Vikings for transport and trade; almost all of them have dragon heads on the bows of the ships.

use your gagging spell in case he misses. He can't conjure up when they are gagged."

The crowd of adventurers was crouched near the entrance, waiting for the eventual battle. The *Karvi* was inching toward the shore with each stroke of its oars. The mage seemed to be telling a few of the Orcs some instructions as the boat was about in two-foot-deep water, but they seemed to be arguing about something. Finally, one orc splashed ashore and went to investigate the rowboat stranded on the shore. The other Orcs shook their heads and refused to jump into the frigid waters. The one ashore came back with a shrug of his shoulders and got back onboard the *karvi*. The occupants of the longboat were furiously arguing, with the mage seeming to be the leader, but they didn't budge. The mage conjured up a Scryer eye and directed it up and down the coastline. Eventually, the boat back-paddled away from the shoreline, turned to the right, and slowly oared up on the coastline. "Whew, that was close," whispered Stefan "Let's get the hades out of here as fast as possible." As the sun was already set to expire, the group abandoned the cave and scampered to the top of the cliff. They made good time running and walking fast until they had put some distance from the shoreline. They still had to keep an eye on the skies above because of wyverns, but at least now the group was able to slow down to a steady walk. Stefan had wandered ahead, parking himself upon a small knoll, where he scanned the countryside. Vulkanfjall was fully visible in front of them, but now they had a chance to get a glimpse of the mage towers. They seemed to be about ten meters in height, made of stone, and fixed upon the top of each tower was a Scryer eye. Unlike the eye of a mage, these were stationary huge eyes—like cats' eyes—rotating on the top of the tower. There were two towers, maybe three hundred meters between them.

Stefan had rejoined the group and, whispering, said, "This is the most dangerous area to be at. We can only move when the eye turns away. We need to time our movement between the eyes' movements. That means that we need to target boulders, ravines, or some kind of cover, run to the location, and wait for the eye to turn away."

The going was slow and monotonous, scampering between the eye movements. "Keep an eye out for the other towers too. Unlike the cave, detection now is certain to bring doom upon us," murmured Stefan. It took the band about five hours to skirt the first tower. "We have about twelve hours of darkness before sunrise. We need to get out of this area. Next tower is up ahead, and I don't know how many more are ahead of us."

It was starting to snow now, and the group applauded the snow clouds. It resulted in the band now making twice as much speed as the pounding and drifting snows helped to conceal them from the eyes. After another nine hours of dashing between covers and the everlasting eyes, they finally had reached the base of Vulkanfjall. What was ahead was climbing and more climbing, so Stefan directed the men toward a craggily area where they could rest and wait until the next sunset.

Castle Vokva

King Bragga was reprimanding Strompur, even before he knew who was. "Dolt! You are ruining everything. Now the humans have every reason to up the ante on the dwarves. How dare you incite the citizenry of this city! Once Gisli returns to HearthGlen with the news of this revolt, we are finished—finished, I say. Put this on top of the assassination, the humans will have no mercy on us!"

"What assassination? What are you talking about? We've killed no one," retorted Strompur.

"So you don't know about it? The killing of the Althing member?" interrogated the King of Strompur.

"Nay, A've not heard of the killing. Thousands of dwarves languish in dungeons and killings of dwarves. I say good for him for dying! At least the killing of one Althing member less is not enough. How dare you! You call yourself a king? You're nothing but a tool for the humans relishing the suffering of the dwarves while you sit on this pompous throne, living a life of luxury! You have seen what the citizens of this city think of you! I curse you for your wicked ways. How many more dwarves do you intend to see in the stocks or dungeons or killed or burnt out?"

"Hrmph, and who am I speaking with? Do you not know that I am King Bragga of Vokva?" asked Bragga.

"Strompur be me name, forgemaster be me trade. And I know you from your evil ways, not as a king. Be civil with your tongue, or I'll have the mobs below have you. You wanted to talk peacefully? Well, out with it then."

"Ahem . . . well, you see, ahem . . . I can still use my persuasion, maybe lessen the punishment against the dwarves. You see—" King Bragga was cut short his sentence.

"Persuasion? You call that a punishment? You for one are the dolt, not me. As long as you sit on this throne, we have been subjected to one offense after another while you are protected by the humans. I say enough! If you do not release all the prisoners from the dungeons forthright, empty out the royal larder to feed the hungry below, then I will not do a single thing to stop the mob. What say ye, o King Braggart?" stated Strompur.

King Bragga was in a spot, and he knew that with a single word, he would be tarred and feathered like Gisli was. Strompur held the high hand in the game of poker between them, and the king was stalling for time. "Aye, p-perhaps I have been a little bit heavy-handed. B-but release *all* the prisoners? Some of them have committed crimes against the kingdom! And empty the royal supplies to-to this mob of lawbreakers?"

"Aye, der be no compromise. Release *all* the prisoners, and feed the people. Else . . ." Strompur threatened the king.

"And your other demands, what are they?" asked Bragga with a stolid face.

"That you leave Vokva. If you love the humans so much, you can go to live with them," firmly stated Strompur.

"B-but this is unreasonable. Who would be king? You? No, I will never turn my crown over to a traitor such as you!" pleaded Bragga.

"Aye, who would be king, ye ask? I wish never to be a king. You can appoint anyone you wish, as long as it isn't you," responded Strompur.

"And you do not object to Germaine as your next king? What if he pardons me and brings me back?" suggested Bragga.

"Me donna care who ye picks, but the peoples here will insist he be honest, with high standards, is decent, and works fer the dwarves," demanded Strompur.

"I will consider what you say. How about three days from now" asked Bragga?

"NAY! Me wants an answer, yea or nay, and I expect it within half an hour," stated Strompur, and with that, he left the castle, returning to the mob below.

Rober was saddling three horses, his and two others. He intended to break Friða and Laugalfur out of the dungeon. After readying the steeds, he used his dagger to remove one of the horseshoes on the other horses in the stable. *They won't be able to chase us down this way,* he thought. He switched to his stealth mode and entered the dungeon. The prison was a damp and moldy place, with little light save for the torches placed on the walls. There must have been fifty prisoners, mostly dwarves and elves, for crimes of debt and theft, and many of them had been there for a long, long time. He wandered around the dungeon until he found the cell that contained Friða and Laugalfur, which had several posted guards before the entrance. Rober sapped the first guard, who slumped to the floor with an "Ugh," and sapped the second guard when the first one hit the ground. The second guard joined his colleague on the ground. Grabbing the key to the cell, Rober entered the lockup, and using his lock-picking skills, he released the manacles around their wrists and freed both Laugalfur and Friða. Both Laugalfur and Friða had been flogged. The bloodstains on their backs were a testimony of it.

"Who's there?" demanded Laugalfur of the unseen Rober. "Psst, it's me, Rober. Keep quiet, or you'll never get freed. We have horses. We need to leave quickly. Grab the weapons from the guards that I sapped," whispered Rober. Some of the prisoners in the other cells were shouting because Laugalfur and Fiða had been freed. "Shut up, you fool. We will be back to release you soon," whispered Rober to the convicts.

They made their way to the stables area, and Rober instructed them to ride like their lives were on the line. He knew that it would not be long before the breakout had been discovered, and the guards knew where to go to capture them again. Soon the three of them were galloping through the main gate to the castle to freedom. Immediately, the alarm was sounded, and the chase party was scurrying to the stables area. The lead guard alerted Remus, and the chase was on. With a missing horseshoe, it wasn't much of a chase. They had to return to the stables area to find a blacksmith to re-shoe the horses. This gave the three escapees about two hours of a head start.

Rober and the fleeing convicts slowed down since they weren't under any danger of apprehension. "Did you know that Helgi was assassinated?" asked Rober of Laugalfur. "That is why I have joined your group, to fight for our freedoms. I want nothing to do with humans, other than my mother, of course. I will do what I must do to reunite the elven clans and other little people."

Friða was shocked, not about Rober joining forces, but that Helgi had been killed. "I-I haven't heard," she stammered. "He was a decent human, full of life and good character. I am so sorry, Rober."

"Aye, Rober, I am sorry too. I know now that he was killed for the little people. I have been shortsighted in many things in my life, but he was a true friend of the elves. Please forgive me for my rash opinions about Helgi," said Laugalfur with sorrow in his voice.

"Best pick up the pace. Once we get into Sko Forest, we can hide out and make plans. Maybe the dark elves will take us in," instructed Rober to the other two riders.

King Aegir had heard of the prison break. It flew like a wildfire throughout HearthGlen. He knew deep inside that it was the actions of Rober. He summoned his court scribe and commanded that he start to set the record straight in writing. He wanted all the revelations about the Althing, all the actions to this period to be disclosed in writing. He knew he had very little time to spare if he wanted to save the lives of Rober, Friða, and Laugalfur. He also commanded that this was the day that will be historical. He declared Helgidagur, in honor of Helgi the Grey, to be a realm day of honor. He further wrote that the Althing was, from this day forward, pending the arrest of the members and that the Althing will resume once elections were held by the populace.

King Aegir had been awakened; he vowed to be a king, not just a figurehead. He addressed the citizens of HearthGlen, calling for calm and that all crimes against the kingdom will be investigated. The king had a difficult time with dealing with the citizenry of HearthGlen. Too much water had flowed under the bridge, and the poisonous rhetoric would have to be repaired, and that would take time. He addressed the crowds and explained that the corruption and greed were the culprits and that Althing had lost its way. He promised to reinstate the Althing once the investigation was over and that the citizens must take good care in electing new members.

After addressing the crowds, he then ordered Jon to bring his armor and weapons and that the royal guards will accompany the king to Fort Hermana to quell the disturbances within the kingdom. The king knew that Remus had formed posses' to go after the elves in Woodbranch and the dwarves in Vokva. The king was worried that Remus would not try to take Friða, Laugalfur, or Rober alive. The elves in Woodbranch would be no match for the armed men; the kingdom didn't need more killings. Remus would be brought back to HearthGlen into custody by the Royal Guards once they found him.

Strompur relayed his list of demands to the crowd assembled around him. He said, "If the king does not reply to our demands, then we should storm the castle." The assemblage murmured their approval when Strompur listed one demand, that King Bragga must leave the city and abdicate. Soon shortly afterward, Germaine exited the castle and strode toward Strompur. "He has accepted your proposal. I trust that he will not be detained or harassed when he leaves," said Germaine.

"You have my word that Bragga will not be hindered in any fashion" Strompur beamed. He turned to the mob outside the castle and announced that no one here must impede them when King

Bragga leaves. Turning back toward Germaine, he asked if he was needed to be of assistance, to which he said no. "As to the prisoners and pantry supplies?" asked Strompur.

"This will be accomplished as we speak," agreed Germaine, to which the crowd threw up a cheer and slapped Strompur on the back.

"Aye, me best be off, going back to Sko Forest," stated Strompur. With a worried look on his face, he announced to the crowd that the little in people in Woodbranch were in dire need of assistance and asked for volunteers. He explained that the little people were working on a plan to leave the human-controlled lands for uninhabited lands across the seas, where the little people could live in harmony with no interference. Strompur received five hundred volunteers!

(Unknown, 2013)

The Cave

Stefan and his gang set out to climb the mountain known as Vulkanfjall as the sun had dipped below the horizon. He needed to contact Traikon to find out exactly where they needed to go, but he wanted to put some distance between the towers and their eyes. Up they trekked, plodding the steep walls of the volcano. It was a terrible climb; their arms and legs were raw from trying to climb the boulders and sheer parapets, which were astonishingly massive. For eight hours, they scaled the objective without any rest, and when they came across a ledge, Stefan decided to rest and to try to contact Traikon.

The group dropped their knapsacks and fell to their backs, relieved for the rest. They ate some flaxen bread, refreshed themselves with water, and engaged in small talk. "I don't relish the walk back to Sko Forest," said Mikael. "Aye, me long ta be in my own bed for a week," added Smapoly. The ledge offered excellent cover from both the elements and the towers. It was cold, but the ledge offered some relief from the high winds. The snows had stopped, and the gang was enjoying the northern lights. "I couldn't make it here without you, guys—kinda like having a bunch of brothers. I hope we never lose contact between us. I wish I had a home to come back to. Blesugrof was the only home I ever knew," said Stefan with sadness in his voice. Mikael put a hand on Stefan's shoulder. "If I had a brother, it would be perfect if he was like you." Stefan smiled graciously and remembered that elves don't talk about family.

Stefan retrieved the amulet and conjured up Traikon. "What are we looking for? Where do we need to go? We are about halfway to the top now."

The spectral Traikon responded, "Yes, yes, I can see you now. Right above the ledge, if you look to the right, you will see a boulder outcropping that resembles a dragon head. Go inside the cave. Follow it down to the end. It is a large cave, so you will have to walk a bit. At the end, there is an indentation on the wall. Place the amulet into the notch and turn. It will deactivate the portal. Oh, I almost forgot, there is an *einauga* that guards the portal. Lots of luck. See you soon."[12] The image of Traikon disappeared, and Stefan whistled softly. "Wow."

---

[12] Einauga: cyclops creature armed with a spiked club.

The group ascended several meters, and they had spotted the rock that resembled a dragon head. They sidled along a ledge until the cave was within sight. "Now, what to do next? Anyone has any suggestions?" asked Stefan to the other members.

"Well, lets me see," said Smapoly "lets us get into to the cave. I can blink around till he kin follow me back to you."

"Blink into the entrance of the cave, maybe someplace in the cave where we can find some cover," instructed Stefan to Smapoly. Smapoly complied with the order, and then he was gone. He returned in a few minutes and said that there were plenty of boulders and such in the mouth of the cave. "Ready, gang?" asked Stefan. "Let's do it then."

The band of adventurers crept into the hollow and waited for their eyes to become adjusted in the light. There were several huge boulders, and off to the left was a ledge, about three meters off the ground. "Sounds like this will be a good spot for an ambush. Smapoly, when I get on the ledge, draw the *Einauga* toward us," whispered Stefan.

After Stefan mounted the ledge, he armed himself with his sword, and with a nod of his head, Smapoly blinked, disappearing into the darkness. For a few minutes, which seemed to be an eternity, a shout from the blackness was heard. "You there, ugly! Catch me if you can!"

The walls of the cavern were shaken with every swing of the Einauga's club, and the air began to be thick with dust. *Clomp, clomp, bang,* as the *Einauga* clumsily chased Smapoly. "Nah, nah, betcha can't catch me," shouted Smapoly. Suddenly, Smapoly appeared next to Stornef, with the *Einauga* standing about fifteen away from them. He was one ugly creature with one eye at the center of his head. He stood perhaps eight feet in height, armed with a huge spiked club in his hand, a dark-skinned creature with a huge mouth and gigantic teeth.

Mikael cut loose with a volley of arrows, and Stornef took a few steps toward the thing with his ax in hand. The *Einauga* was growling and spitting from its mouth and charged the group. Stefan, with his glowing sword in hand, leaped onto the shoulders of the monster, and with his free hand, he had managed to grab a tuft of hair. The *Einauga* commenced to twirl, his arms flailing over his shoulder in an attempt to rid the unwanted passenger, like a horse trying to dislodge a rider from his back. Stefan was pitching from side to side and trying to avoid the arm of the *Einauga* at the same time. Stefan had to lock his legs around the neck of the *Einauga* to prevent having him thrown to the ground. He was stabbing constantly about the neck of the creature while Mikael was bombarding the Einauga with arrows. Stornef fearlessly charged into the affray. Smapoly had an idea: to freeze the area around the entrance then to push the beast over the volcano! "GET BEHIND 'IM! I'll freeze the ground, 'n' you push 'im over the ledge!" With three of the people assailing him from different angles, he became confused as he didn't know which one of the three assailants to target with his club. Smapoly conjured a sheet of ice near the entrance while Stefan was stabbing constantly in the ear of the *Einauga*. Suddenly, in a loud growl, the creature slipped on the ice, and Stefan released his hold as the *Einauga* fell into oblivion. The gang could hear the monster careening off the mountain with thumps and crashing's. Stornef grabbed Stefan to prevent him from falling, and the two of them sat on the ground, all out of breath. "Whew, that was a fantastic plan!" Stornef shouted.

After everyone had recovered from the assault, they ran to the back of the cave. Stefan retrieved the amulet, inserted it, and the portal instantly appeared, glowing and swirling greens and blues within it. Traikon stepped out of it with a breath of freedom. Suddenly, Traikon yelled, "We've been discovered!"

Strompur, with his five hundred volunteers, needed to skirt Fort Hermana on the way to Woodbranch. Off to the right, they could see the torches' lights on the horizon from the humans as they advanced toward Sko Forest. "Ride with the winds!" shouted Strompur to his followers. "We 'ave no time ta waste!" He knew that they needed time to set up a credible defense force once they reached Woodbranch. *What do we do once we get there? The children and women need be evacuated to safety,* thought Strompur. *At most, we 'ave 1,003 warriors, 'n' I'll fight the humans to the end if I 'ave ta.* Strompur was worried about Rober and Stefan and his crew. If the quest for Traikon was successful *and* came in time to be of any use to the little people, then maybe . . . perhaps Strompur was full of wishful hope.

Woodbranch Revisited

Rober, Laugalfur, and Friða rode nonstop throughout the night, taking a detour toward the seacoast to avoid the humans around Fort Hermana. Laugalfur was having a problem with keeping up due to the lashing he had received while in the dungeon. Every stride of the horse was painful, but he never complained. Friða wasn't too bad since she only received a minor lashing because she was a woman. The three of them were silent for the most part, hoping to reach safety within Woodbranch. "We're almost home. Just hang on. I'll get you some help with your wounds. Mother and Father will try to heal you. Just hang on," Rober pleaded Laugalfur. Friða began to admire Rober for his heroics toward the elven clans; she no longer thought of Rober as a half-breed, and she had come to accept him as a true elf. *Björglin will need help with adjusting and fitting in within the clan. Funny how the world is turned upside down. Our best friends, Helgi—a human—and the dwarves and gnomes, plus now Rober and his family . . . yes, I will try to change my thoughts of them,* thought Friða. *Poor Björglin. It must be horrible to be despised by her own kind and the elves. I shudder to think what the humans will do to her if they catch her. Rober has changed our lives forever. He didn't have to rescue us. He put his own life in danger for someone who hated him.*

It wasn't very long before they had reached Woodbranch. Rober dashed to help Laugalfur off his steed, hollering for help. Gjaldakona went running to greet them, hugging her daughter. Runar and Björglin rushed forward and helped Laugalfur to Gjaldakona's home. Everyone was hammering them with questions about the humans: where they were and how many of them were. "Did you hear about Helgi?" "What about Stefan, did you hear any news?" Endless questions, but no time to answer them.

Rober fell into action; he began to organize the defenses, directing elves, gnomes, and dwarves where to go and what to do. "If this is our last stand, I want to die with honor and dignity among you people!" shouted Rober. "Fret no more about Helgi. He is where he wants to be. Fight for Helgi the Grey, the one true friend of the little people!"

The humans had reached the outskirts of Sko Forest. Between the trees, they could hear the angry shouts of the mob and see the glistening of torches between the swaying branches. "GIVE UP LAUGALFUR, FRIÐA, AND ROBER!" shouted Remus toward the forest. "GIVE YOUR CRIMINALS TO US, OR WE WILL BURN DOWN THE FOREST. THIS IS YOUR LAST WARNING!"

Rober shouted back, "COME AND GET THEM, YOU SNIVELING COWARDS!" And with that, a volley of arrows flew from the forest toward the humans.

Remus cursed and yelled, "CHARGE! BURN THEM OUT! KILL EVERY SINGLE STINKING ELF!" The mob charged blindly toward the forest, setting ablaze some of the trees, shouting and cursing at the same time.

The elves stationed within the forest peppered the lead row of humans with arrows, dropping three or more of them. The mob, mostly farmers and peons, stopped the advance and ran back to where Remus was. Fully enraged, he scolded the humans. "You cowards! I said attack those disgusting elves! Do as I command you! Burn the forest down!"

As the elven coven was bracing for another assault, Strompur and his army of volunteers emerged from the left of the mob. "ATTACK! Don't let 'em burn down the trees!" yelled Strompur. The horsemen of dwarves charged into the mob, scattering them about. Several humans fell in battle, causing confusion and disarray, to which the mob began to run back to safety. Then they spotted the soldiers from Fort Hermana charging toward Strompur and his men. "RETREAT! To the forest!" commanded Strompur. He knew that the well-armed and trained soldiers would make quick work on the raggedy group of volunteers. Strompur found Rober amid the forest, standing next to Friða. "Looks like the end for us," said Strompur.

Last Stand

Stefan was distraught because the game was up. Now they had no way to return to Sko Forest let alone of getting down from the volcano. Between the mage towers and the wyverns and the marching Orcan soldiers, there was no way they could escape. "Now what do we do? Traikon, you promised to bring the little people to a promised land. Do you have a suggestion?" beseeched Stefan.

"Tut, tut, no problem," answered Traikon with a sly grin on his face. Without hesitation, he transformed himself into a dragon! "I'll call my children to help us out. Hop on, and hang on!"

The group just stood and stared with unbelieving eyes. Smapoly gulped and uttered, "Not again. Me be a-scared of heights!" It wasn't long before hundreds of dragons, old and young, appeared in the skies above. One of the dragons had landed and picked up Stornef and Smapoly on its back, and Stefan and Mikael rode Traikon. "Ready?" asked Traikon.

"What about the dwarves and gnomes in Vokva?" asked Stornef.

"That is what my children are here for. They fly as we now speak," answered Traikon. With that, the band of adventurers took to the sky. Smapoly, being held by Stornef, squeezed his eyes shut, his body shaking from his fear. Below them, the ground had been lit by scryer eyes, and a few wyverns took to the air, but they were never any match for speed, distance, and height against Traikon and his children. They seemed to marvel at how little the orcs were as seen at this height, as though they were harmless insects.

Vulkanfjall was fast disappearing from sight as Cloister Bay came, with its majestic icebergs and occasional whales, and they went flying by, leaving the bay behind them. Traikon turned to the right toward Fort Gate-Pass. Stefan marveled about the stories he had heard about the glorious battles that had taken place there; the sagas and heroes sprung to his mind so long ago as a child. Below them was the Blafjall Mountains, with its snowcapped peaks and passes. Stefan and his crew were elated that they could soar upon the backs of the dragons, like angels reaching out to save the little people. They were astounded that it only took an hour through the air while it took three weeks when trodden by foot. *I clearly recall the last few months: the drudgery, the killings, the bitter cold, and brushes with death. It seems like a dream now,* thought Stefan as they flew onward to Woodbranch. *I only pray to the gods that we are in time.* On they flew for another hour; off the left was the Lava Gate Pass. What a magnificent sight! The infamous gates, constructed many centuries ago, were now broken and lifeless. Someplace around here was the famous Jarnsmiða Forge—the ancient dwarven citadel now destroyed by earthquakes and eruptions from the Eldfjall Volcano. Stefan was astounded by the rich historical locales and their influences on the inhabitants of this world. *I guess Traikon wasn't joking. We will be famous. A making of history, I guess,* reflected Stefan to himself. Up ahead, they were nearing Fort Hermana, and beyond lay their destination. Off to the right would be Blesugrof but not visible from here. He was guessing, but the party should be landing in another fifteen minutes.

Strompur ordered his men to spread out and use as much cover and concealment as they could find. He was waiting for the dreaded attack of the soldiers. All of a sudden, Rober ran to the edge of the forest and taunted Remus. "You are a disgusting piece of filth. You're a liar, a cheat, and a murderer. Come and get me, you fool, if you can!" Rober yelled, and slipped back into the brush. Remus blew up on that, waving a fist at Rober. "You have been sentenced to death at my own hand!" screamed Remus, to which he unsheathed his sword and rushed forward. With Remus yelling at the crowd behind him to follow him, a dozen humans reluctantly joined in. The soldiers from Fort Hermana were about thirty paces behind them.

"What in the world did you do that for?" screamed Friða to Rober.

"'Tis a good day to die for my friends and family," responded Rober. "Kill as many as you can, then flee to the dark elves. May be the gods with me!" He rushed to meet Remus.

Suddenly, a horn was sounded with a shout of "Cease and desist! Your king commands you." The armies from Fort Hermana stopped their advance as the king rode between the ranks toward Remus. "I command you to take no action. Sheath your weapons. That's an order!"

The farmers with Remus were confused, and because they were not soldiers, they hesitated and finally ran from the battle. "Remus! I am placing you under arrest for corruption and murder. Drop the weapon and surrender peacefully."

Remus refused the command and screamed at Rober, "It is your entire fault! You've ruined my destiny, you disgusting elves!" He raised his sword over his head and charged Rober. Rober had no difficulty with Remus's attack. He was more agile, and with his training from the rogue guild, he easily sidestepped Remus. "Face me, you coward," screamed Rober to Remus. "Fight like men. Defend yourself, unlike Helgi, who was killed at your command." Rober sheathed his daggers and taunted Remus with a wave of his fingers. Remus struck out with his sword toward Rober, but he was too slow and clumsy. Remus again swung his sword, which Rober parried easily, and Rober struck him the jaw with a fist. Remus staggered back, screamed, and resumed his attack. Rober unsheathed his daggers and threw them into the chest of Remus. Remus dropped his sword, gazed in astonishment at Rober, tried to say something, and collapsed to the ground. Rober retrieved his daggers and strode into the clearing, followed by Friða and Strompur.

With that, Traikon landed between the king and Rober and his allies. Stefan threw him off the dragon and ran toward the king. The royal guards brandished their weapons to protect the king. "Hold. No need for more killings," ordered the king and turned to the mob and soldiers from Fort Hermana. "Go home. There will be no more killings today. You men from the fort, return to your posts. Rober, step before me. I am still your king," commanded the king.

Traikon returned to his human form while Stefan ordered Rober to stand his ground. "Your Highness," said Stefan as he knelt on one knee. "I agree that there have been too many killings this day. Much has occurred in my absence, and I wish to speak forthright with you."

"You must be Stefan, brother of Rober. Speak, and I will give you consideration with what you have to say," stated the king.

"I have come to beseech you to let our peoples go. We no longer wish to be a part of this kingdom.

I also want you to empty your dungeons throughout the kingdom of gnomes, dwarves, and elves for their alleged crimes. With all respect, Your Highness, we elves, gnomes, and dwarves too have suffered much. The injustices against our peoples will not cease, regardless of how many arrests of the perpetrators. I humbly ask that you keep our dignity and honor by letting us go," avowed Stefan.

Rober interceded and said, "We will fight to the end against the oppressions which have been brought upon us."

The king rubbed his chin for a moment. "And is Runar here? What does Runar have to say? Rober, I am as much pained as you for the killing of Helgi. I do not consider you an enemy of the kingdom. I have ordered the Althing dismantled and the perpetrators arrested."

Stefan was shocked as he had not heard of the killing of Helgi. "H-Helgi is-is dead? H-how can that be?"

"I am as sorry as you are, Stefan. He was a true friend of mine. Runar, step forth and address your king," demanded the king. Runar, with Björglin in hand, went forth and approached the king. "What say ye, Runar?"

"We are all in agreement. We need to leave the kingdom," concurred Runar.

The king was solemn faced; he dismounted his steed and approached Runar and Björglin. He took Runar's hand in his and said, "Runar, my friend, I-I grant you your boon. But before you leave, let it be known that Sanctuary City will be a priority as long as I am king. I wish a boon from you in return. Stay here and become the first ambassador to Sanctuary City."

The cheers were deafening, the backslapping, the kisses and tears of joy—there was much work to do.

6

EXODUS

Woodbranch had never experienced an event such as this: the gnomes, dwarves, and elves dancing, laughing, crying, and elating. Runar and Björglin had accepted the offer from the king, and now they were enjoying the reunion with Stefan and Rober. The day was filled with happiness but, at the same time, mourning; they were mourning for their beloved Helgi the Grey. The ales and *landa* were flowing freely within the coven grounds, and the sorrows of the past seemed to have been disappeared. Rober excused himself as he wanted to be alone. Gjaldakona was cackling with glee as she talked with Friða, Laugalfur, and Traikon. The gang of adventurers wandered around, eventually winding up around the campfire in the middle of the coven. Stefan and his crew—Mikael, Stornef, and Smapoly—were sitting around the campfire, enjoying their pipes and gulping down mugs of ale. Only one person was missing from the crew, whose original task had brought them all together: Rober. He was standing in the forest on the outskirts of the coven, sullen and downtrodden. Björglin watched as Rober seemed to be sobbing, so she wanted to console him. Of the death of Helgi the Grey, Rober had been influenced more so than the others. Björglin placed a hand on his shoulder, but she didn't know what to say to him. "My son . . . my dearest son . . . I-I wish I could make everything all right again. I used to be able to make everything go away when you were a child—sing to you, hold you, and comfort you. I know the pain in your heart. I so want to ease your pain," she said with sorrow in her eyes and voice.

"Mother, the world has turned its back on me. The things I used to enjoy in life are gone. It has been filled the emptiness with anger, bitterness, and rage. I have killed people," sobbed Rober. "I have stolen, I have lied, and I rejected my king. I suppose that I blamed Aegir for the death of Helgi. I have been thinking about many things. How I long to flee to the new lands, but how can I flee from myself?"

Björglin wiped a tear from her eyes and grabbed her son and hugged him tightly, kissing his head. "I know, my son, I know. Such is life—many things that you have no control over. Sad to say, but some things can never be undone."

Stefan looked around for his mother and found her with Rober in the edge of the forest. He joined them, and he detected a feeling of sadness sweep over him. "Mother, Rober, are you feeling all right? Gjaldakona was out by the campfire a little while ago. She wanted to thank you. Oh, Laugalfur too. He shook my hand, and he wanted to talk to you."

Rober wandered within the coven until he had found Laugalfur. "How are your wounds?"

"Great. Stornef used his healing powers, and they are almost gone. But as for you, are you doing all right? I-I want to apologize to you in person for the things I have done and said against you. I am truly sorry," expressed Laugalfur. "I now know that my insolence has caused you and your family much grief. Take my hand as I offer to you as a friend, a friend for life."

Rober smiled at Laugalfur and grasped the extended hand. "I too wish to be a friend in life. I now know that I was trying to be a human and an elf at the same time. I am more elfin then human, and I am proud to be an elf."

Laugalfur beamed in satisfaction after he heard Rober's words. "We need to organize the clans, for there is much work before us. I trust you that you will be coming with us to the new land?"

"Aye, there is nothing here to keep me now," answered Rober. "Why don't you ride out to the dark elves' clan, invite them to join us? They are still elves, and we need them as much as everyone here."

"I would love to reunite the clans, and it is all because of you and your family," exclaimed Laugalfur.

Smiling, Rober asked where Mikael was. "I have one more request of Mikael."

Laugalfur said that he was in the home of Gjaldakona, and with that, Rober departed to speak with Mikael.

Answering the knock on the door, Gjaldakona cackled with a smile on her face. "Come in, Rober, please do come in."

Inside, he was stunned to find Friða there—dressed as a siren, clad in the prettiest dress. He never had seen her except when wearing warrior's clothing; she was stunning to see. She had let her hair down, adorned with a wreath of flowers upon her head. Her eyes twinkled like stars; she was a beautiful woman. She looked at Rober, just beaming with happiness; their eyes locked in adoration. For a moment, Rober saw no one in the room except Friða. Mikael cleared his throat, which broke the spell, causing him to recognize Mikael. "Ah, it is wonderful to see you again, Mikael. I haven't spoken to you in what, a month or so?"

"Aye, 'tis good to see you too," answered Mikael.

"And you, Traikon, I must confess that for many years, I always thought you were a fantasy. To that, I apologize. Mikael, I have one more request of you," said Rober.

Traikon gracefully accepted the statement from Rober; Mikael agreed to any request from Rober.

"Do you remember the goblins and Loftur? Can you ride out there and extend an invitation to them to join in with the journey to the new land?" asked Rober.

"You are wise beyond your age, Rober. I had almost forgotten about them. Of course, I will depart immediately," stated Mikael.

Friða began to speak as Rober's heart leaped to his throat; the voice from her was magical. "I have never had the opportunity to thank you for your saving of our lives and your devotion to the clans." Without warning, she clasped her hands upon his hand, fell forward a bit, and kissed Rober on his lips. Rober was totally taken aback; he stuttered, clearing his throat, with absolutely no words coming to his mind.

Traikon broke the ice in the room by saying, "Well, shouldn't we fly out to your new home?"

Our New Home

Traikon had switched to his dragon form and had summoned two additional dragons to his side. Everyone agreed that the first ones to view their new home would be Stornef, Mikael, Smapoly, Rober, and Stefan. Everyone cheered as Traikon and his crew of dragons took to the air and watched until they were out of sight. Runar gathered the leaders of the clans to make plans for the big move. There would have to be construction crew for housing, the castles, docks for ships, and a thousand other goals that they wished for. Slowly but surely, the stream of would-be settlers began to stream into Sko Forest. The newcomers would need adequate housing, food, and chores to help with the move. It was a daunting task as they didn't want to damage the forest, so the appointed leaders needed to travel to Fort Hermana to get permissions for usage of the available lands. Of course, the shop owners didn't mind the extra business, as the signs of *No Gnomes, Dwarves, Elves, and Dogs Allowed* were with replaced with *All Newcomers Welcome*. Eventually, there formed a committee to help with the new settlers, directing them to suitable places and assigning them to various tasks. There were hundreds of ex-prisoners who had been paroled, many of whom had not seen their families for ten years or so. Just trying to keep up with who was where and what they were doing was a gigantic chore. The wagon trains stretched for miles, laden with little people and their families and their possessions. Everyone took the inconveniences in stride; pride and a sense of dignity made everyone smile.

The next day, the dragon riders returned; they were immediately mobbed with a million questions. Stornef had tears of joy streaming down his cheeks; it was indeed a paradise. He recounted the mountains teeming with gems and ores for the dwarves to work; Smapoly was telling the other gnomes of the green pastures perfect for animal husbandry, and Stefan was swamped with questions about the lush and boundless forests. Friða never left the side of Rober, talking of the new freedoms and their futures. Woodbranch had become a hub of bees' activity; everyone was courteous, helpful, and for once after many years, happy. Traikon appointed a group of dragons that conducted daily flights between Vokva and HearthGlen.

As time passed, the docks were constructed on the North Sea coast, making the transportation of men and materials easier between the lands. Even the dark elves and Loftur and his goblins pitched in with the effort. Runar and Björglin were frequent visitors of HearthGlen, coordinating things with the king. Runar, Laugalfur, and Gjaldakona even visited the new lands, which they called Helgilands. Even the ban from using the name Agnar had disappeared as Runar had told the complete version of his great-grandfather. The new forests for the elves became Agnarborg to honor the efforts between the dark elves and the Woodbranch elves during the Rending Wars. The dwarves had appointed Strompur to be the new king once the castle was built, naming it StrompurForge. The elven clans offered the kingship to Stefan, which he declined. "I have done nothing heroic, nothing of worthiness to the clans. I therefore wish to honor the one person here with that title: Rober!" Due to this, Rober was anointed to be the first king of the Agnarborg for the elven peoples. Strompur set aside some caverns in the mountain area of Helgilands for Loftur and the goblins.

Years passed, and slowly but surely, Sko Forest returned back to a normal forest. The elves had relocated to Agnarborg, the dwarves to StrompurForge, and the gnomes transferred to the pasture lands of Helgilands. The docks in the North Sea became a thriving fishing village, and the commerce between the Southern Realm and Helgilands was flourishing. Sanctuary City was finally completed, and Runar and Björglin were established as the ambassadors. King Aegir also returned Blesugrof to Runar and his family in honor of their accomplishments. He also established Sko Forest as a realm forest, prohibiting any commercial use there.

Some people say that Mortikon had been recalled by Óðin for breaking the pact with the Referees.[13] It is told by some that Mortikon was banished from the world and sent to an ice-filled exiled place named Mortieyja. Prince Maura assumed control of the Northern Realm, and King Aegir finally gave up his throne, naming Jon as the king for the Southern Realm.

King Aegir had a difficult time with reestablishing the Althing, but in the end, the citizens of the Southern Realm accepted Althing as a political body. The king was tired and getting old, and he wanted to live his remaining years as an ordinary citizen.

As for Able, he had eluded the dragnet from the scandals from the Althing. He has never been seen or heard from again.

The murder of Helgi the Grey was never solved. There were numerous suspects; however, no one was apprehended for the crime.

Mikael settled down in the forests away from Agnarborg as he chose to live with the dark elves' clan. He married and had six children.

Rober married Friða, and they were superb as reigning king and queen over Agnarborg and bore four children: two males and two females.

Strompur and Anna managed to return the dwarves as powerful allies with the elven clans. They brought back the pride and honor, which had been lost in the past.

---

[13] Óðin: Odin or Wotan, king of the gods.

Smapoly became a wealthy business owner in his own right.

Vokva is still ruled by Germaine although its stature and influence had diminished considerably. StrompurForge still has daily flights between Vokva, but most dwarves prefer to live in Helgilands. Now the only dwarves left in the Southern Realm are just a token number.

As for Svaramin, little is known other than he died as a broken-down old wizard in an undisclosed wizard's tower.

Traikon moved in with Gjaldakona with numerous trips between Agnarborg and the caverns where the dragons set up their lair.

Sanctuary City was an outstanding success, and to this day, it is still operational.

Time moves ever slowly, but it does not stop. Over the years, the day of honor for Helgi the Grey morphed from Helgidagur to the term still used today: holiday.

The End

BIBLIOGRAPHY

Domain, C. P. (unknown). *pixabay-33877*. Retrieved from
   Pixabay: www.pixabay.com
domain, p. (n.d.). *Pixabay warrior metal-43159_150*.
   Retrieved from Pixabay: www.pixabay.com
Domain, P. (Unknown). *Photobucket Elven Warriors*.
   Retrieved from Photobucket: www.photobucket.com
Domain, P. (unknown). *pixabay*. Retrieved from
   pixabay—32253: www.pixabay.com
Domain, P. (unknown). *Pixabay*. Retrieved from
   Pixabay—31630: www.pixabay.com
Domain, P. (Unknown). *Pixabay*. Retrieved from
   pixabay—48840: www.pixabay.com
Domain, P. (Unknown). *Pixabay 46745*. Retrieved from
   Pixabay: www.Pixabay.com
Domain, P. (unknown). *Pixabay thief man-43511_150*.
   Retrieved from Pixabay: www.pixabay.com
Domain, P. (unknown). *Volcano black-32829_150*.
   Retrieved from Pixabay: www.pixabay.com
Unknown. (2013, Unk Unk). *cave-35194*. Retrieved from
   Pixabay.com: www.pixabay.com/35194

MAPS

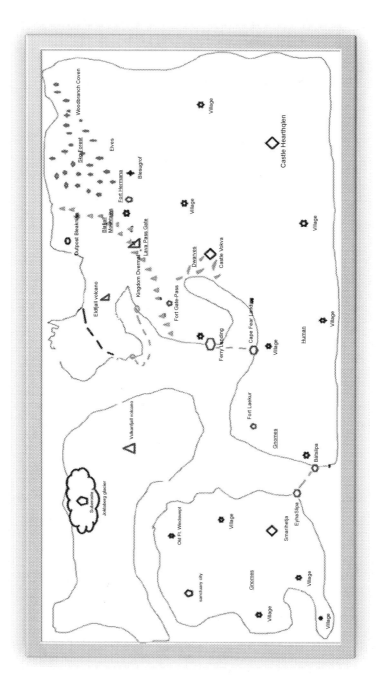

Northern and Southern Realms

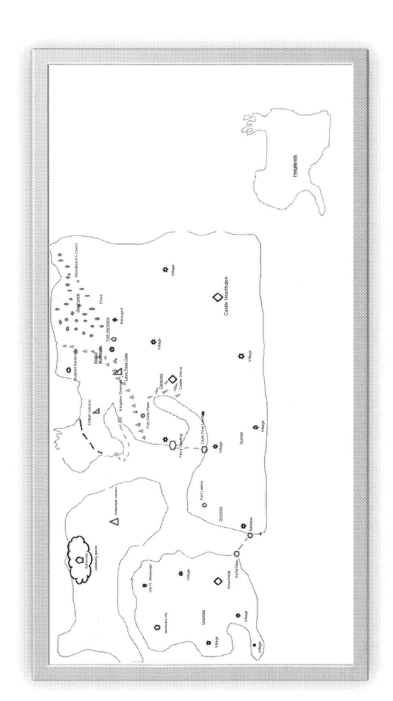

Northern and Southern Realms and the new land, Helgilands.